FATAL

USA TODAY BESTSELLING AUTHOR
TAYA RUNE

RIGHT TO RULE SERIES

USA TODAY BESTSELLING AUTHOR
TAYA RUNE

Purple
Realm

PUBLISHING

Taya's Steamy Books

Steamy Contemporary

Champagne Resolutions

War of Hearts

Bewitching Twisted Fairytales

The Charming Thief

Fantasy Romance
The Right To Rule Series

Outcast

Lethal

Fatal

Betrayal

Denial
(Coming January 2024)

<u>Paranormal Mystery Romance</u>
Enchanted Underworld
Weapons of the Fae Queen Series

The Warlock's Lair

The Oracle's Court

The Nymph's Realm

The Dragon's Garden
(Coming 2nd November 2023)

Check out her website for all her current works.

tayarune.com

Newsletter

To receive up-to-date information, news and exclusive
offers online please sign up for the
Taya Rune newsletter.

https://www.tayarune.com/subscribe

Content Warning

If you are concerned about content, please check Taya's website for a list of warnings for all of her books.
It can be found under the 'Books' tab.

tayarune.com

For Roxanne
My ride or die xox

Prologue

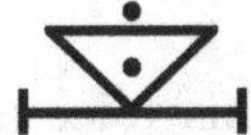

A horse and cart rumbled past Zussya as he walked toward the waiting figure. It was too dark to make out the man's facial features, but his height was difficult to hide; even leaning against the wall his shoulders hunched against the night, and even with one hand resting on the shiny handle of his fancy cane it was clear this man was tall. The royal genes continued to breed true.

"Thank you for coming; I wasn't sure you would." The Arch Deacon spoke quietly as he approached the man.

"I was curious." The man's voice was aloof.

Arch Deacon Zussya had kept tabs on this young man since the moment he was born but had only had the opportunity to meet him a few times. His mother had very much kept him isolated and away from anyone who might give him a different truth.

"I was given something eighteen years ago, in the hope it would never need to be delivered. But you have chosen your course of action so here I stand." Zussya held out the small, folded envelope.

"What is it?" The young man pushed himself off the wall, and straightened his shoulders. Zussya surmised he was probably the tallest out of the three brothers.

"It is a letter from the Seer, written before she left eighteen years ago."

"That ungrateful bitch. I doubt this letter has anything trustworthy written in it." The man spat to emphasize his disgust.

Zussya frowned and his voice hardened. "You may be a prince, but you would do well to remember who you speak to and about. The Gods appoint the Gifted and she is the only one in three generations to wear that brand. Do not offend the Gods," he warned.

"Mother says the Seer would not do a reading for her as she was working for the usurper and in cahoots with that traitor Evannderth. Mother believes the Seer didn't want to admit to having a vision of something that would not agree with the future everyone wanted."

"Your mother," the Arch Deacon emphasized the words, "drugged and imprisoned Lady Kahlahnni to use her to her own advantage. Captain Evannderth uncovered this and rescued the Seer."

Prince Tommofey raised his voice and several people looked around. "That is not true!"

"Keep your voice down," commanded Zussya. "Do you want the palace gossips knowing your business? No? Then don't draw attention to it." The Arch Deacon shook his head, for all the young man was a prince, he had a lot to learn. Being tall enough to draw people's attention, even in a nation of tall people, was not his fault, but adding to it by standing here with an ostentatious cane and raising his voice was one sure way to get noticed by anyone walking past the palace walls tonight.

"You lie about my mother and expect me to be quiet about it?" There was heat in the prince's voice.

"I will not stand here and qualify my opinions on Lady Darria. I was charged by the Seer, eighteen years ago, to give you this when or if you chose to pursue your mothers ambition of putting you on the throne. She appears still hellbent on the choice, even if it could cost you your life, and I am assuming so do you."

"Do you know what it says?" Tommofey asked suspiciously.

"No. I would not break the trust of the Seer. What you do with this will be up to you. Once you take this note, my duties will be discharged."

"Fine." Prince Tommofey snatched the proffered note. "Now, you can go." His tone was dismissive and rude.

Arch Deacon Zussya paused and raised one of his heavy, brown bushy eyebrows at the young man, astounded at his audacity. "Perhaps in your mother's pretend palace you get away with such poor manners, but out here in the real world it would serve you well to remember that a kind word will always get you further than a harsh one. Ruling a nation is more than just ordering people around. The Lady Darria was once known for her compassion and warmness; I am appalled to think her bitterness and need for revenge has reached such levels that she has forgotten who she is at her core."

The young man bristled but did not respond.

Good, thought Zussya, *he does have enough control to not retaliate further.*

"I will bid you goodnight, Priest." The haughty prince inclined his head and moved away without waiting for a response.

Zussya didn't hurry away, he waited and watched as Tommofey walked with his shoulders back, using his cane in a way that was purely for show, drawing people's attention intentionally. He reached the next hanging lantern along the palace wall and paused to have a group of soldiers assemble around him. The Arch Deacon shook his head, this man wanted to be seen, he wanted everyone to know who he was and to be talked about. But why?

The sound of his own stomach gurgling interrupted his musings and reminded Zussya that it was well past his dinner time. He would have to grab something at the tower when he got back. There was always bread warming by the ovens, and cheese and cured meats available from the kitchen.

It had been a long afternoon seeing Prince Harlonngraith off with Evannderth through the portal to find the prince's Champion, and now delivering Lahnni's message to Prince Tommofey who had created the need for the search of the Champion, by challenging his half-brother's right to rule. But the day wasn't over yet, for now the planning began. There were six months until both parties were required to arrive at the Arena. A Challenge had not occurred in centuries that Zussya wanted everything to be researched thoroughly, he did not need anything missed, nor going wrong.

As the Arch Deacon began to walk back toward the palace gate he had come from, he decided that he might kill two birds with one stone this evening by seeking his dinner and checking on Prince Platisse at the same time. The youngest and most studious out of the three princes, Platisse lived in the tall spire tower that housed the nations Brothers of Seggar, as did the Arch Deacon. Platisse had been sent to study under Zussya many years prior, which had been wonderful. Zussya had had someone to share his knowledge with and had found Platisse willing to always spend time researching whatever was required of him. But overtime, Zussya's responsibilities had continued to grow as the Cardinal in charge of the Order's health faded and Platisse spent more time in the library pursuing his own interests under the guidance of the others. They weren't as close as they once were, but Zussya felt compelled to check in with the prince tonight. After all, it's not every day your brothers embark on a journey that will see one of them die in six months at the hand of the other.

Chapter 1

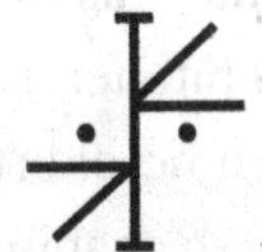

Tommofey

Prince Tommofey knew the walking cane was a bad idea a quarter of a turning into his journey to meet Arch Deacon Zussya. By the time he had completed the boat ride across the wide river that separated the twin cities, and made his way to the assigned lantern on the outside of the palace walls, he was ready to hand the cane to the captain of his personal bodyguard, Albertinne. But he was stubborn, too stubborn his governess would say. Stubborn enough to hold onto that cane even though it was chaffing his palm and he would end up with blisters. Tom did not like to admit he had made a mistake, he would rather suffer through the consequences, even when it was unnecessary or painful.

As he entered his suite, finally alone, he tossed the cane onto the chaise lounge with too much force and it bounced off the padded cushion and hit the serving tray that held a pewter ewer filled with red wine, matching goblets, and a covered tray of sweetmeats. The lot ended up on the floor, which Tommofey completely ignored and left his page, Griggory, to deal with.

The prince continued through the outer lounging area and into his private bed chamber; off to the side was a screened area where he changed from his heavy over cloak into a soft robe that was in his favorite navy blue. He poured water from a pitcher into the basin he used to wash himself from when he didn't want to be bothered visiting the old palace bath chambers, and dipped a cloth in before placing it on his raw, chaffed hand. Tom swore savagely as the sting of the cool water hit the warmth of his hurt hand.

With a moment of hesitation, Tommofey went to the cloak that lay crumpled on the floor and took out the note. He held it with two fingers, like it was dirty and poisoned, and walked to his personal writing desk in the corner of his bedchamber. He preferred to work from this one, rather than the larger one in the outer lounge area that was piled high with things his mother felt he needed to know about on how to run a nation once he became king. His personal desk, that no one but Griggory saw was uncluttered, with a neatly stacked pile of varying sized rolled parchments on a small table. They were all maps. Prince Tommofey had a thing for cartography that no one knew about.

The seal that held the letter closed was still intact and held the symbol of the Gifted. He mused that one day he too would have a wax seal that no one but him in the entire nation would have. The Monarch brand was almost as unique as the Gifted one. That would hopefully make his mother finally happy—her wish to see him crowned king come true.

Tommofey stopped his daydreaming and took up the fancy letter opener on his desk. He carefully slid it under the pale blue wax blob and broke the seal. The note was short, no more than a few paragraphs, which for some reason disappointed him.

Everything I see between you and your brother is finely balanced. Regardless of what you are told, I only see for the good of the person and the nation. Something is hidden, lurking, waiting. If you continue on your course and take the throne, it will remain hidden; if your brother reigns, what is hidden will be revealed. Whatever is hidden is dark and dangerous.

I have seen the location of both the Champions. Your brother has left on his quest and now it is time to leave on yours. If you have not changed your mind once reading my warning, you can seek your Champion to the Southeast. On the edge of the country facing where your father perished while hiding rather than ruling.

Learn your lessons well, it may be the only thing that saves us all.

Tommofey frowned as he read the final sentence twice more. What was it supposed to mean? This was all twisted messages with no true meaning. Just like his mother had warned him.

He dropped the note onto the desk and went out to pour himself a glass of red, only remembering that he had spilled it everywhere when he found Griggory madly scrubbing the rug in an attempt to remove the large stain.

"Leave that, one of the maids can deal with it in the morning, or we can replace it. Have more wine brought up, and cake. I feel like cake," Tom announced. "And see if my mother is still awake, I would like to see her if possible."

"Yes, Your Highness." Griggory stood and bowed hastily before hurrying out the door.

The prince retied the sash to his robe as he moved back into his bed chamber to retrieve the note. He brought it back out with him and sat on the chaise lounge, rereading it several times, while he waited for his page and word from mother. It wasn't long before there was a polite knock on the door and his mother calling his name. "Tommy?"

Prince Tommofey opened the door and smiled down at his mother. She was lithe, fair in color, but with brown hair. "Mother? I could have come to you."

"I was up and didn't need all the message sending; much easier for me to just come to you." She reached up and patted his cheek with affection. "Is everything okay?"

"Come in, I need to talk to you about something and don't want to discuss it in the hallway." Tommofey stepped aside to let Lady Darria through.

"Well, you have definitely made me curious," she said as she followed him into the room. "Oh my, what happened here?" She stopped as she saw the red stain on the rug.

"A small accident."

"Ah, Pages can be a little clumsy, especially when they are going through a growth spurt."

Tom didn't correct his mother. "He is replacing the wine and getting cake. Would you like a pot of tea brought up?"

"Oh yes, if we are having cake, tea is perfect."

He went to the door and opened it and looked at one of his personal bodyguards who stood outside. "Mother wants tea; see to it."

The man saluted and began to walk away. Tommofey didn't bother to watch, he returned to his mother to find her standing in the room, the Seer's note in her hand. "Where did you get this?" she asked, her voice a little shaky.

"That's what I wanted to speak to you about. Arch Deacon Zussya sent me a message yesterday requesting a meeting. He mentioned that it would be in my best interests to see him as the Challenge has now officially begun and as of today I am allowed to begin my search for my Champion." Tommofey led his mother to the high backed chair, closer to the fireplace and well away from the red stain, so her satin slippers wouldn't run the risk of being stained and ruined.

"And you went to this meeting without telling me?" Her voice was waspish.

Tommofey refrained from pointing out he was an adult and no longer needed her permission to do anything. After all, in six months he would be the King of Segarris and would not be seeking her consent for anything. "I didn't want to bother you and I took my guards. I was safe," he assured her.

She continued to frown but nodded. "Go on."

He went to speak when there was a light tap on the door. "Come in," he said loudly.

Griggory opened the door, carrying a large flagon of red wine. He stood back but continued to hold open the door for the two women that followed. One carried a silver tray with tea making paraphernalia, while the other carried a covered platter that Tommofey presumed held his cake. He waited patiently while the servants did their job. The two serving women left and Tom sent Griggory to bed. His small room was off Tommofey's bedchamber.

Once the tea was made, cake cut, and wine poured, they both settled into their chairs by the fireplace. "So, you met with the priest?" Darria prompted.

"Yes, it was a brief meeting. He said he had been keeping something for me for eighteen years and had been instructed to give it to me only if you and I went through with challenging Harlonngraith's right to rule. He said it was from the Seer and that he had never opened it."

"Anything else?"

Tommofey paused for a moment; he didn't know whether he wanted to ask about what she had done to the Seer. Finally, his curiosity won. "He said that you drugged and held the Seer captive." Tom didn't ask if it was true.

"Did he now?" She didn't answer the question.

They both sipped their drinks and waited.

"Well, I suppose it could have looked that way. I just wanted more information. She kept saying basically the same as what was in that note. That everything was too even, she couldn't see your future. I didn't believe her and I think her disappearing the way she did makes my theory more believable."

"Why?"

"You know I think my horrid sister got rid of the Seer because she did see something when Evannderth stole her from me and took her to the fake queen. I think she saw you winning and Anzhellika couldn't deal with it and had her killed. I think Evannderth was killed too, to cover the whole thing up."

"Then where did the letter come from?" mused Tom.

Darria took another large bite of her cake. "Maybe she learned about the letter and that was the final straw? Maybe the letter is fake, and you are deliberately being led somewhere else in the hope you fail at finding your Champion."

"So, you don't think I should consider figuring out the clues the note says I should look into?"

"Don't you think it is a little too convenient that it shows up now?" countered Darria.

"Of course I do, I am not an idiot. But to be honest, I don't know where else to start. Do you have any ideas?" He looked pointedly at her.

"Well, no. Do we have any information on what Harlonngraith is doing?"

"As I waited for Zussya, I watched Harlonngraith ride out with his personal guards and enough pack horses that it was clear he had made a decision on where he would begin to look."

"Damn, I did not expect them to act so quickly."

"The priest said he got a note too. If the Seer is truly doing what is right, and it is all too finely balanced then would it not stand to reason that Harlonngraith would also receive a note with instructions?" Tom argued.

"Yes, but that means we are putting faith into two people we have no grounds to trust," Darria reminded him.

Prince Tommofey drained the rest of his goblet and put down his cake plate. "Shall we revisit this in the morning? Perhaps we should sleep on it before making any decisions that will affect my life expectancy?"

He bid his mother goodnight and escorted her out his door, watching until she had entered her own suite down the corridor. He looked to one of his bodyguards and nodded before closing the door and latching it.

As Tom walked back into his bedchamber, he looked over to his pile of maps. The instructions the Seer had put in the note kept rolling around in his head. Tommofey went to his desk and selected a map and carefully rolled it out, putting weights on each corner so he could look at it without holding it flat. He traced his finger across the map, repeating the words of the Seer.

Seek your Champion to the Southeast. On the edge of the country facing where your father perished while hiding rather than ruling.

He did the calculations. If the location was right, the time it would take for him to get there and be back to the Arena did not give him much leeway to dilly dally. Decisions had to be made.

It was only turnings later when he lay awake that night, struggling to sleep, that he finally realized if the Seer wrote the note eighteen years ago, she had predicted the King's death and no one had known.

Chapter 2

Aviva

T he horse snuffled at her overcoat pocket, and she absently pushed his nose away while continuing to comb his beautiful chestnut mane with her other hand.

"Stop that," Aviva muttered.

He snorted his disagreement and nudged her to make his point. "Not until I am finished." She laughed. This was the favorite part of her day. When the meal had been prepared and served, the two other girls who helped in the kitchen offered to finish up the washing so Aviva could help in the stables. She had once asked why they did this for her most days, sometimes even twice a day, and they had admitted she was less grumpy with them if she got her fix of horse. And as they all shared a room, it was a compromise they were willing to live with. Aviva knew she should have felt guilty for making others' lives difficult, but she was so happy to be in the stables she didn't really care.

Her life was lonely. Aviva found it difficult to make friends, most found her bluntness jarring. She had never truly conformed to the norms society required, and her only family member was away most of the time. Spending time with the horses was the only thing that made her happy. She was trying to be a little less cranky with the girls, but didn't always succeed. Her sharp tongue didn't always help either.

At twenty-two, Aviva had been at the garrison the longest, the other two having only received their brands one and two years ago. Her father had been the swordsmith on the main island of Lobbregath, Pluddgish, in the large Segarris garrison that housed the soldiers sent to protect the citizens. Her mother had died when Aviva was seven, and when the marauders of Trioswa began their summer raids that year, her father could not protect her and Shai and do his job, so he sent them to the garrison on the coast of Segarris. Binttle sat on the high bluff of the mainland overlooking Pluddgish in the far off distance.

Aviva had never returned to Main Island and her father had perished a year later in a raid. The siblings had remained in the care of the garrison in Binttle, but had been put to work to earn their keep, until their brands had been given and they had been moved to their preordained positions in life.

"There you go, handsome." Aviva patted the neck of the horse and put the comb away before returning with her promised treat. She took the pilfered carrot from her pocket and snapped it in half, giving the stallion one piece and pocketing the other. He snuffled at her coat. "No, greedy boy, it's for your brother." She gave him one final pat before leaving the stall and closing the door carefully behind her.

Aviva would never make that mistake again; it had been the reason she had been caught in the stables in the first place. Thankfully, when Stablemaster Darvell had seen her trying to coax the three escaped horses, who were now casually milling in the center of the stables, back into the stalls, he had shown her how to do it rather than report her for sneaking in and letting them out in the first place.

"You done, Viv?" The owner of the beautiful horse entered the stall.

Aviva nodded to the soldier in his immaculate uniform. "Yes, he's all ready for afternoon patrol."

The soldier stepped back and studied his horse. "You do know you don't have to brush his tail and mane each time we go out?"

"Do you brush your hair every time you go out?" she retorted.

This made the soldier laugh and flipped her a small bronze coin. "You have a point." He touched his forehead to the horses and stroked its neck. "You do look handsome once Viv is done with you. Shall we go catch some bad guys?"

Aviva caught the tossed coin and held it tightly in her hand. She would stash it later, once she was alone. She stepped out of the stall to allow the soldier to mount and lead the stallion out. Aviva closed the door once he was on his way and moved to the next horse that would be needed. This gorgeous boy was the same chestnut coloring as his brother, but he had a cute white patch that ran down his chest.

"Oh, Viv, I almost forgot," the soldier called out. She turned to see he had stopped and was looking at her over his shoulder. "Housekeeper says to get your tail up to the kitchen. There is a double patrol of men headed back from Main Island today and you are expected to pull your weight."

Aviva went to protest that she always pulled her weight, but he held his hand up to forestall her.

"I'm just the messenger."

She bit back her smart retort and forced a smile.

"Thank you."

Aviva walked into the next stall and murmured a greeting to the horse while offering him the half carrot. She slipped the coin into a pocket on the inside of her coat. "Hello, big boy." Aviva reached up and scratched behind his ear. "Enjoy your carrot; I can't stay today." She sighed heavily, "There's a double patrol of soldiers coming in from Main Island." Viv mimicked the soldier, suddenly pausing when she realized what she was saying. Her sullen mood lifted as she became more hopeful, gave the horse a final scratch, and hurried back to the kitchen.

Aviva burst through the kitchen's double doors and almost knocked over a boy who was gingerly carrying a tray with a cup of milk on it, his tongue sticking out to one side in an effort to concentrate. Aviva hurried to the Housekeeper in the far corner who was sitting at her desk and issuing orders while resting her bloated leg on a stool. The older woman, who treated everyone like they were her family, smiled knowingly as she saw Aviva come storming across the kitchen. "Ah, I see ye decided not to dawdle today."

"Is it true?" Aviva asked, clearly eager for what she hoped would be good news.

"That there are men coming home? Yes?"

Aviva nodded.

"I have two of the girls opening up the windows and putting out clean linen to ye brother's troops rooms, if that what ye are asking about."

She let out a loud whoop. Her brother was coming home.

Chapter 3

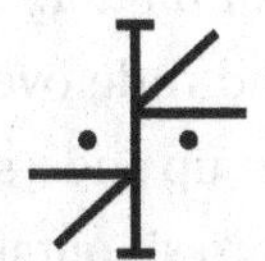

Tommofey

Prince Tommofey and Lady Darria had wasted almost a month deciding on whether to follow the Seer's note. In the end, it had come down to them not having an alternative on where to look for his Champion that Tommofey had got his mother to begrudgingly agree to follow the Seer's instructions.

Prince Tommofey and his entourage had been on the road for five weeks and he was finding the experience challenging. He had not realized how much he had relied on his mother until she was no longer there. He had never had friends, always preferring the company of his maps and he had been raised to trust no one. Everyone, in Lady Darria's opinion, had an ulterior motive.

He sat on his horse, Toby, impatiently waiting for his tent and furniture to be erected for the night. He was hungry, tired, and a little lonely. But what weighed on his mind more than anything else was how he would find his Champion. It was all fine and well to follow the words of the Seer, but she had not advised him of anything other than what location to look in.

"Your Highness, your quarters are ready," Captain Albertinne announced as he strode toward Tommofey. "Would you like to bathe or to have your dinner first?"

"I'll bathe while I await dinner."

Tom nudged Toby and rode over to his large pavilion. There was an awning set up and a small table with a chair, in case he would prefer to sit outside, as the weather had been pleasant all day. Tom dismounted and handed his reins to the groomsman who had been assigned to care for Toby and walked into the tent, grateful that the severe aches and pains of sitting in a saddle all day had finally abated. The first week on the road had been hideous, and it had taken all of Tom's acting ability to dismount and stride into his tent without moaning or limping.

Even though it was still relatively light outside, the large tent had several lit lanterns for him to see by. The pavilion held a small writing desk that he used for his meals, a large, padded mattress with several blankets and cushions, a tiny, low table that sat by his bed, and a draped off area that was allocated to his page, Griggory. There was a thick pile rug on the ground that helped keep the chill away at night.

While Griggory set about unpacking belongings for Tommofey's bath, the prince stood in the center of the tent and stretched slowly. First he reached his hand up, feeling the easing of his aching shoulders, then swung his arms down and bent forward. He couldn't touch his toes, but every day he did this exercise he got closer. Standing upright, he swivelled his torso from side to side before finishing by lunging forward on each leg and then moving back to stretch the back of his thigh. By the time he had completed his stretches there was a polite cough outside the tent. Griggory hurried to let the soldiers in that carried the round tub that the prince used for his baths. It wasn't ideal with his larger frame and height, but it was enough for him to soak off the dirt from the road each night.

After the past few weeks, the prince and his page had settled into a routine while they waited for the water to be brought up from the river they were following, the fires to be built, and the water to be heated. Tommofey sat at the small desk and waited for Griggory to bring him the precious carry case that he carefully placed on the table. The page was not expected to unpack the case, as the contents were too valuable and Tommofey didn't want the boy to accidentally break or spill anything.

Tom undid the buckles that held the lid in place, and almost reverently lifted the soft leather encased top to reveal his most treasured possessions. His cartography set. He pulled out a velvet-wrapped item and gently un-folded the fabric to reveal a small journal that he had been taking all his notes in, as well as drawing each section they travelled throughout the day. He hoped when he returned home, after he was crowned king, he could have all of the single page maps merged into a large and far more accurate map than the current one they had at the palace. Well, his palace anyway. There was a high likeli-hood that the official palace where his half-brothers had grown up held a far more impressive map of Segarris. He looked forward to seeing it once he won the Challenge.

After placing the book to his right, Tom took out the small pots that held his different colored inks and the fine quills that he used to create his drawings. There was also a half-sized ruler and a magnetized compass, which had been a gift from his father. Tommofey had been fascinated from the moment he was presented with the compass and explained its use. The final items he took from the case were a set of small paint brushes made of sable and a tiny dish with a little lip that he filled with a few drops of water from his flask. After placing the now empty case at his feet and arranging things on his limited work space to his liking, Tommofey lost himself in creating a map of what they had experienced for the day.

His anxiety melted away and his mind sharpened to recall every detail in his notebook to match the picture he had drawn. Today they had travelled beside one of the large main rivers that supposedly spanned the length of Segarris. Tommofey had always immersed himself as a lonely teenager in the notions of following the rivers and discovering all their secrets, and if in fact they did span the continent. Those daydreams had been slowly overtaken by his mother's want for him to prove himself as rightful heir and ascend the throne of his father. The leisurely hours studying maps had been swallowed up with tutors of every kind to prepare him to rule.

By the time he set his work aside to dry, his bath was ready and Tommofey quickly disrobed and sank into the mid-chest high tub. He leaned back and allowed Griggory to lather his light brown hair and massage his scalp, before rinsing himself by sliding into the hot water. Once his hair was done, Tommofey took the fine smelling soap from the boy and lathered himself before handing the bar back to be set aside to dry and be repacked. "Go find out how much longer I must wait for supper," he ordered Griggory. The waif of a child, with his darker coloring, depicting that he came from the Southern province scurried from the room leaving Tommofey alone with his thoughts.

The prince rested against the side of the tub as best he could, wishing that he could stretch out a little more, but his long legs would not allow for that. Being tall had many advantages, but sitting in a cramped tub was not one of them. He hoped the meal that was being prepared was a little more exciting than the salted ham or fish he was being forced to eat on the nights they were not near a town. He missed his rich five-course meals at the palace, and had noted when he got dressed that morning he had had to tie the sash around his waist a little tighter than normal.

Griggory coughed politely, startling Tom as he must have dozed off. "Yes?" he spoke gruffly.

"Your Highness, tonight the cook has prepared you rabbit stew. It will be ready in a quarter turning."

Without being prompted, the boy fetched a towel and held it out while Tommofey stood and let the water drip from him for several moments before stepping out of the tub. "Rabbit stew sounds appealing. It is still pleasant outside, I shall dine out there."

"They are running drills, Your Highness," Griggory mentioned.

Tom waved his hand dismissively. "Your concern is noted, but not needed. It will give me something to watch while I eat. These four walls certainly lack for entertainment."

By the time Tommofey had dressed, Griggory had set the small table under the tent awning. As the prince settled into his cleverly crafted collapsible chair, that he always felt was never built to take the weight of his heavier frame, he nodded for the boy to pour him a goblet of the red wine from the travel barrel he had packed. A metal bowl of rabbit stew was placed before him, with a chunk of warmed bread resting on the side. Tommofey nodded in satisfaction and his mouth watered with anticipation as the smell wafted upward, reminding his stomach that it had been a long time since the midday meal.

The sun was setting and he noted the darkening clouds skimming towards the camp. *Wonderful,* he thought to himself, *just what I need to deal with...rain.* His thoughts were sour. He wished he had someone to talk to. These were the times he missed his mother the most. She was always good for witty conversation, and palace gossip. Though, as time went on he was starting to appreciate the peace that came with no longer having to hear about the continuing feud between his mother, the cast-off queen, and her sister, the current queen of Segarris. It was as if her every thought circled back to that and so must every conversation.

As he sat quietly and ate his rabbit stew, the only sound intruding on his meal was the clash of swords and the grunting of his guards as they sparred. He watched the two men circle each other and it brought his thoughts back to why they were here in the first place: to find his Champion. They were still many weeks away from their destination, but each night, as Tom went to sleep, his last thoughts were of the pressing matter of once they arrived how would he find the one he was looking for?

Chapter 4

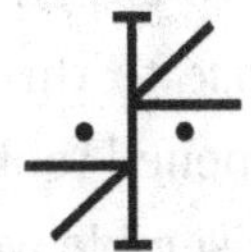

Tommofey

The weather had soured, and it had been drizzling for several days. Prince Tommofey was in a foul mood as they approached the large town's paltry gates. He was sick and tired of the mud and feeling soggy. The fact that he still had no idea how to find his Champion was taking up his every thought. The pressure was building and he still had no idea how he was going to find the one person on this continent that would be the one destined to fight to the death for him, and most importantly, be good enough to win. Though, he did consider that if this was all in the hands of the Gods, why did he have to work so hard and endure so much to find this person? If he was supposed to be the one, why did the Champion not just present himself at the gates and make everyone's life easier?

"Your Highness." The mayor of the town that Tommofey couldn't recall the name of at that very moment bowed deeply. "It is an honor; we did not expect for you to visit us. Lodgings have been arranged for you and your page at the best inn. It would be my pleasure to escort you there myself. The Lieutenant here will show your men to the garrison."

"That sounds suitable." Tommofey didn't bother to wait for Captain Albertinne to assign bodyguards, they had been doing this for close to three months now and it worked like a well-sharpened tool. All the prince wanted was to get out of this miserable weather.

Toby began to follow the tall, slender mayor who wore a heavy ermine cape to keep the rain off, though Tommofey wondered how he kept it from rotting and stinking. He suppressed a shudder.

Two guards, Griggory, and the prince followed the mayor and his small entourage of people, whom Tommofey hoped he wouldn't have to be pleasant to for much longer, trudged through the puddle-filled street to a surprisingly large and well-appointed inn with a boar painted on the low hanging board.

"Welcome to the Dancing Boar," announced the inn keeper as he bowed slowly, then stepped aside for the bodyguard to enter first and check the common room.

After more fawning and surveillance, Tommofey was settled into the only two room suite, usually used by rich traveling families. Griggory busied himself unpacking his prince's clothing and belongings while Tom sat at the round dining table, that could have easily sat eight, and hummed softly to himself as he took out his cartography kit.

The night passed pleasantly and Tommofey was woken by a small tapping on his door. He waited for his Page to answer it, but after a few more taps, realized that the boy probably could not hear the knocking as he had been assigned the smaller bedroom further from the door. Sighing in frustration, Tom threw the warm blankets off and threw on a robe that the inn had provided. He padded to the door and pulled it open. "Yes?" he asked.

The bodyguard on the other side looked startled and quickly saluted. "Your Highness, your meal has arrived."

The prince stepped aside and allowed the serving maid holding the covered platter into the room. "What happened to your face?" Tommofey asked, as he noted the swollen eye of his soldier.

The seasoned warrior turned red. "Lucky hit by one of the garrison's guards."

"You were fighting the town's soldiers?" Tommofey asked.

"Sparring," he corrected.

This statement surprised the prince. "You do this each time we come to a town?"

"Yes, sir. The troop know each other's strengths and weaknesses very well, this way we practice against new opponents, and it keeps us fresh. It's become a bit of a competition amongst the men; we haven't been bested, yet," the soldier explained with pride.

"It is good to know that my safety is in capable hands."

"Your Highness, would you like me to set the table?" asked the woman who had placed the tray on the table.

"No, that is fine," he responded distractedly, an idea was forming and he wanted her to leave so he could think on it further. "My Page will see to my needs."

He waited for her to curtsy and leave the room and then turned back to the guard. "Send for Captain Albertinne," he ordered before closing the door.

Prince Tommofey hummed happily as he removed the cover from his meal and prepared to break his fast. His mood buoyed by the idea forming that he didn't bother to reprimand Griggory for sleeping in when the boy came out of his room rubbing one eye while tucking in his shirt.

Aviva

Aviva looked sourly at the pile of pots she had been assigned to scrub as punishment for sneaking out early from dinner service last night to tend to the horses, rather than deal with the stupid banter and innuendos from the returned soldiers. Aviva silently counted the pots. Twelve disgusting pots, with baked-in cruddy bits on the bottom. It was going to take her forever.

You know what to do to pass the time, she told herself as she started to place the pots on the clean empty bench. The kitchen would be empty for about half a turning as the servers and cooks had their breakfast in the large common room now that the soldiers had been fed and were about their day. Aviva took the large kettle from its hook over the stove, too impatient to let it come to the boil and poured enough warm water in the bottom of each pot to cover the baked on gunk. With disdain, she picked up the small scouring brush and dragged the over-sized pot to her. As she began to scrub, Aviva allowed her mind to wander.

It had been a difficult few months. Nothing had gone the way she had hoped, and it had put her out of sorts, wanting more and more to escape to the quiet stables where the horses loved her and were happy to see her. Her chores had increased as the number of soldiers who had returned was substantial. It appeared that approximately half the soldiers that had been stationed on Pluddgish, the main island on the Lobbregath Islands, had been ordered home. It was a surprising thing to do, but everyone hoped that it signified that the end of the Trioswa Marauders was close at hand and peace was coming. Though, it was muttered by the older men that the peace never lasted more than a few years. Aviva had secretly wished that she had a way to discover why the Trioswa constantly sought dominance over the Lobbregath Islands. What was behind the constant raids that had taken her father from her?

As a child, she and her brother had whispered about their dreams of owning a farm somewhere on Segarris when they were older while they were hidden in the room of their father's smithy when Pluddgish was be raided. They swapped stories of how she would breed and raise beautiful horses while he tended the gardens and helped out the neighbors to keep their minds off what was happening outside. When Aviva had been shipped off to the main garrison in Binttle with her brother while their father stayed behind, they would spend their dark cold nights planning how they would earn enough money to buy a small farm, escaping from the life they were forced to live. But everything had changed when Shai had been branded a warrior, set to join the ranks of young men sent to train and then come back and die on the cliffs protecting the Main Island of Lobbregath.

Aviva had thought all their dreams shattered when that brand had occurred, but before Shai left for training and each time he had returned, they had continued to plan and save for the day when he could be discharged and they could follow their hearts and find peace.

Still to this day when Aviva couldn't escape to the stables to find solace, she sunk into daydreams about her life on the farm with her brother. As she tackled the stubborn stain on the bottom of the pot, Aviva imagined how different her life would be in a few more years. She would have saved her share of the money and they would be free to find a safe homestead where she could cook, clean, and take care of the horses because she wanted to, not because it was required.

After rinsing the pot and setting it aside to dry on the edge of the brick work that surrounded the large fire in the kitchen, she went to work on the second pot. Though Aviva tried, she couldn't keep the persistent thought that her brother had changed and was avoiding her because he no longer wanted the same dream. It made her feel more than uneasy, but every time she broached the subject he made up an excuse to leave and scurried from the room. He was not the same man who had left over a year ago, and Aviva felt more alone and isolated as Shai now spent most of his non-soldier hours with his friends at the local tavern, never once asking Aviva if she would like to join him.

An excited nattering of voices could be heard approaching and Aviva ducked her head and concentrated on the pot in her hand. She was in enough trouble without being caught daydreaming too. The door opened and the talking ceased for a few moments.

"Have you heard the news?" a young female voice asked. She seemed to be brimming with excitement.

Aviva looked up, curiosity getting the better of her. "No, what news?"

"No one knows."

Her first instinct was to call the girl a twit, but she bit back the snarky comment and instead smiled pleasantly and looked to the other girl. "Do you know what she is talking about?"

"One of the city gate guards came rushing in, waving a note and mumbling something about a tournament."

"A tournament? What else?" asked Aviva.

"That's the thing," the first girl interjected. "No one knows any more than that. The whole place is ablaze with rumor."

"The general has called for an assembly in the town square. There will be some sort of announcement."

Aviva looked at the ten pots she still had to wash. "What time is the assembly?"

"Half a turning."

There was no way Aviva was going to get all the pots washed as well as get to the town square in time. "Can you come back and let me know what they say? Please?" she added.

The second girl, Nikkitta, who was always quicker to forgive Aviva's outbursts, looked at the pots waiting to be scrubbed. "Let me help. Between the two of us we should get it done, and if we run we should be able to get to the town square in time."

Aviva looked at her gratefully. "Thank you."

They began to vigorously scrub the pots. "Oh, very well. I'm not going without you so move aside" Lyubbov elbowed her way between them. "With three of us we won't need to run to get there on time. I don't want to show up red-faced and sweaty," she declared.

It took the three young women no more than a quarter turning to complete the task and they all quickly rushed to their shared room to tidy their hair and change their aprons to clean ones. They arrived in the packed town square just as the herald called for silence by blowing the long trumpet he carried. The crowd hushed immediately and waited for General Alloshenka to climb the stairs. He was old and it took him a few minutes to get there. Aviva wondered how they were ever supposed to hear his words now he had lost the power in his voice. Then she noted Drill Sergeant Fabbron following the General up the stairs. *Smart,* she thought to herself. She was sure you could hear Fabbron from anywhere in the entire garrison, so the town square should be no problem. The general was possibly just here to lend his authority to the announcement, which made it even more intriguing to Aviva.

Drill Sergeant Fabbron wasted no words as he held aloft a piece of parchment before he brought it down before him. "Prince Tommofey has issued the Challenge for his Right to Rule as the only son of King Tommofey and Lady Darria." His voice echoed across the silent townspeople. "He travels to Binttle in his search for the warrior who will be great enough to stand as his Champion in the Arena. A tournament will be held, and all competitors are welcome. The victorious Champion will be paid handsomely for their service with ten times their weight in gems and gold."

The assembled townspeople gasped at the reward and no one could hear anything further as everyone began to speak at once. Aviva waited and watched, an idea quickly forming in her head. The crowd was finally brought back to silence by the herald blowing the trumpet several times and the Drill Sergeant hollering for everyone to settle down.

It was only when everyone had finished shushing everyone else did he continue. "Prince Tommofey arrives in three days, and the tournament will be held on the fourth day, Rest Day, so everyone can attend. There is to be one day of tournament where anyone who wants to compete can. It is a knockout system and the winner, if acceptable to the Prince, will become his Champion and represent him in the Arena. If the Champion wins, he will receive his reward. Any weapon is acceptable. Any brand is welcome to compete. Any employer who stops their worker from competing if they so choose will be severely punished. A proclamation with all details will be hung in all the usual locations if you want further details. You may go."

Drill Sergeant Fabbron didn't stay for questions that would inevitably be shouted at him, he turned and walked down the stairs slowly, while the teetering General Alloshenka followed.

Aviva's mind raced as she was engulfed with the rising noise and shoving of people as they all talked and tried to make their way from the square at once. She took no notice of anyone as her mind went over what had been announced. She started to grin as she thought about her brother and the fact that he was considered one of the best swordsmen in the Segarris army.

Chapter 5

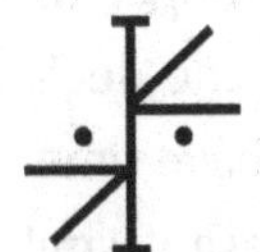

Tommofey

The prince looked at the square, squat town, and wrinkled his nose in disdain. The whole place was depressingly boring. The drab buildings matched the drab skyline making the entire town and its surroundings feel heavy. Rather than focus on the exterior, Tommofey reminded himself of why they were here: his Champion was supposedly somewhere within this town.

As they approached the low-walled city, a welcoming party could be seen waiting for them. Prince Tommofey straightened a little in his saddle and tugged his vest down, wishing it would sit properly. Over the last few months with all the travel and lack of his usual extravagant course meals every day the prince had dropped some weight and his clothes no longer fit properly, which simply wouldn't do for the heir to the throne. He had determined that while they were in town he would have his clothes altered or purchase new ones if he could not find a suitable tailor.

The road they traveled was dusty and dry and the soldiers were constantly clearing their throats. Spreading out to each side was brown grass in need of a good soaking. The scenery was completely uninspiring and Tommofey hoped that his plan worked, and they wouldn't have to stay here any longer than necessary. By taking so long before making the decision to follow the Seer's instructions, he didn't have time to waste.

Tom plastered a pleasant smile on his face as he approached the welcoming party. They bowed deeply and Tommofey nodded at them. "Your Highness, welcome to Binttle. I am Mayor Fenkkston. Please follow me and I will take you to the garrison."

Tommofey frowned. "The garrison?"

Mayor Fenkkston faltered in his stride and turned back to the prince. "Yes, Your Highness. We assumed that you would wish to inspect the troops and to see where the tournament will be held."

"Very good." Tommofey nodded, though he couldn't think of anything more pointless. He didn't care what the troops looked like as long as he found his Champion amongst them.

Prince Tommofey looked at the assembled troops all standing to attention in their neat rows. There was not enough space for him to walk up and down the lines without jostling anyone. "Why are there so many soldiers here? Should they not be out patrolling the Islands that my father died to protect?" His tone was harsh, but he didn't care.

The mayor looked like he wanted the hard packed earth to swallow him whole, but General Alloshenka nodded his understanding and answered Tommofey. "Your father worked hard for this moment. It took a further decade but we have now fortified Pluddgish enough and put in place higher and clearer watch towers so that many of our troops could come home for a rest after many years of dedicated service."

Tommofey felt his anger subside slightly at the older man's words. He looked up at the two story buildings that surrounded them on three sides. The fourth side was made up of a wide, low building where his horse had been led to. "This area is far too small to stage a tournament. It barely holds all the men. Where do you expect me to sit and oversee the competition? There is no shade."

Mayor Fennkston's face turned a bright beet red. "I, uh," he stuttered.

"This is hardly an auspicious start to such an important event," Tommofey pointed out. "I am assuming there will be men from the outer farms and the city itself wanting to compete?"

"Yes, we are expecting an influx tomorrow morning before the tournament begins."

"And where do you propose to put them all?"

If it were possible, Mayor Fennkston's face turned a brighter hue of red. "We assumed that they, of course, would not all be required to be in here at once."

"Well, of course." Tommofey barely refrained from rolling his eyes. "But where will they wait?"

"I, uh—" He again stuttered. "It was suggested that we use the grass plane outside of town and build a platform for you to sit upon," he admitted.

"And why didn't you? That sounds like a far smarter idea." The prince was astounded at the lack of forethought by the mayor. Thankfully he wasn't in charge of the garrison and it was run completely autonomously from the rest of the large town.

"We didn't have much notice to prepare," Mayor Fennkston attempted to explain.

"You have two days to get it built. I am certain with so many soldiers here, returned from active duty, it will not take that long." He turned to the old man in his well-pressed uniform. "General Alloshenka, please liaise with Captain Albertinne regarding how the day will be run. This delay is to be the only one. I must be back on the road and on my way to the Arena with my Champion in four days."

General Alloshenka nodded. "Everything will be ready."

"Good, now, can someone show me to my quarters?"

"I believe that Housekeeper Ottilie was put in charge of preparing the general's quarters for your arrival." The mayor looked expectantly at the wrinkled soldier.

"I beg your pardon?" Tommofey assumed he hadn't heard Mayor Fennkston correctly, not giving anyone else time to speak. "I am not a soldier; I am a prince." He stood his full height and placed his fist on his hip. "My Captain will be here with the men. My Page and I, as well as several bodyguards, will be in your finest inn, not taking up room in this clearly over-packed space."

The prince fumed. How disrespectful. Once he was king, Tommofey would have Mayor Fennkston removed from office due to his clear sheer incompetence and the insult to the crown of expecting the prince to sleep in anything other than the most well-appointed room in this entire hideous town. He couldn't imagine that the general's room held any kind of luxury. Where was he expected to bathe? With the common soldiers? How utterly insulting and ridiculous.

Without further conversation, he spun on his heels and headed to the stable.

"**W**here's my horse?" he demanded, looking around the well-appointed open area.

"Your Highness, if you would wait here, I will have your horse prepared." An older man limped toward him.

Prince Tommofey gave him a look of disdain; the man could do with a shave and a haircut. "Just point me in the direction of my horse." With any luck Toby hadn't been tended to yet and wouldn't need to have his saddle put back on.

"He is just this way, but if you would wait here..." The man pointed to the right and Tommofey didn't give him the chance to continue, he marched over to the doors of the stall and pushed them open.

A loud yelp greeted him as he met resistance to the door opening. "Stop pushing, you buffoon, clearly there is someone on the other side," a female voice said angrily.

What on earth was a girl doing in there? A few seconds later she called out, "You can open them now."

Tommofey frowned but pushed open the doors. Toby stood in the middle of the hay filled stall, lazily slurping up water from the trough and taking no notice of his rider. His saddle was off, and the woman was holding his blanket. She was attractive. About five-foot, eight-inches tall with mid brown colored hair that was being held back by a tan kerchief. One wayward curl sprang out from under the kerchief, and she tucked it behind her ear. Her eyes were an amber brown and currently hard as agates as she glared at him. She had a flush to her rounded cheeks and a small smattering of freckles across her pert nose.

"You need to have him saddled up, we will not be staying," the prince ordered.

"He needs rest," she countered. "It looks like he has been on the road for some time, and he needs to be tended properly."

"How would you know that?"

"I beg your pardon?" Her voice rose an octave.

There was something about this woman that rubbed him the wrong way. It could have been the insolent way in which she glared at him. He was not inclined to answer a commoner. "I want my horse ready to ride immediately. Do as you are told or pay the consequences." His tone was haughty; Tom found that it typically worked to get him what he wanted. He stood on one side of Toby while she scowled at him from the other side.

"And you are?" The wench demanded in an insulting tone, but before he had replied she went on. "Actually, never mind. I don't care who you are. You clearly lack manners and I will not be spoken to in such an insulting way. You don't get to threaten me. Saddle the horse yourself." And with that, she threw the saddle blanket at him and stormed out of the stall.

Prince Tommofey stood there fuming. This town was obviously backward and lacking in graces. In his opinion, this did not bode well for him finding his Champion here. He was beginning to have grave doubts about following the Seer's guidance.

Chapter 6

Aviva

An excited buzz filled the streets of Binttle, but all Aviva could do was worry. She hadn't seen her brother since breakfast yesterday. She tried to appease her thoughts by telling herself that he more than likely had been carousing a little too much and had missed his breakfast this morning in preparation for the tournament today. When Aviva had found Shai after the tournament had been announced, he had readily agreed to compete in the hope of winning the place as Champion for Prince Tommofey and being a step closer to having enough money to do with whatever they wished. Their dreams of owning the farm were much closer, and it had released her worries that he no longer wanted that.

But now the morning had arrived and he had not shown for breakfast and no one could tell her where he was. The staff who worked at the garrison would all be leaving shortly to help serve the soldiers and anyone else who was competing. Aviva hoped to sneak out to the stables before that and ask around. The men who worked in the stables were the ones who usually knew all the gossip before anyone else for some reason, and she would take advantage of it today. If she could just sneak out.

Finally, the dishes were washed, the mess area cleaned and the staff were preparing to leave, but there was still no sign of Shai. "Where are you?" Aviva muttered under her breath as she hurried to her room to change her apron for a dry one.

Lyubbov was already in their room, brushing her hair and pinching her cheeks.

"What are you doing?" Aviva asked.

"Making myself presentable." Lyubbov preened in the mirror a moment longer and checked her teeth. "Can't find me a husband if I look all dishevelled now, can I?"

Aviva shuddered violently, expressing just how she felt about that statement. "Married? Seriously, why would you want to do that?"

"Why wouldn't you?" Lyubbov countered.

"Ah, easy. It's just someone else thinking they can tell you how to live, what to think, and needing to be taken care of."

"Yes, but what about them taking care of you?"

"I don't want to be taken care of. I want freedom to choose my fate."

Lyubbov made a face. "You are so unromantic."

"Romance has nothing to do with it."

Nikkitta came barging through the door, interrupting their conversation. "Housekeeper wants to know why you are taking so long. Everyone is ready to leave."

Lyubbov picked up her bonnet and tied it with a flourish. "Ready."

Aviva held her stomach and grimaced dramatically. "I think I just started my menses. Tell her I will catch up."

They both looked at her doubtfully, knowing she had only finished her last cycle just over a week ago, but neither were rude or brave enough to call her a liar to her face.

"It's your head." Lyubbov shrugged, and they both hurried from the room. Aviva knew they would be talking about finding husbands for the entire walk to the tournament field, her clear deception forgotten quickly.

She picked up her own tired looking bonnet, with its frayed lavender ribbon, and jammed it on her head. It clashed with the red and tan over apron she had quickly pinned on, but she didn't care. Tying it up, Viv hurried down the corridor and turned left instead of right and headed out a side entrance to avoid everyone heading to the tournament.

Without incident, Aviva arrived at the stables to find a stable hand, but instead found Stable Master Darvell bringing out Daissi, a gentle, black coated mare, past her soldiering days, but perfect for the general to ride. "Thought ye might show up here." Darvell grinned at her.

Aviva's heart sank. Him being certain she would come looking for her brother means something had happened. Shai had been acting so oddly since coming home, it was hard to reconcile her memories of her brother to what he was behaving like at the moment. "Where is he?" she asked.

"Rumor has it he was drinking at a tavern last night, doing a little gambling when a brawl broke out."

"And where is he now?"

"Locked up. It seems ye brother had a few choice words to say about the man he was gambling with, and the man's friends took offense and threatened him. And well, we all know ye brother."

Aviva snorted. "Yes, Shai can't back down from anything. He's so stubborn sometimes."

This statement brought a loud laugh from Darvell. "Sounds like someone else I know."

"Very funny." Aviva made a face at him. "I'm not that stubborn."

The stable master raised his eyebrows so high she thought they might disappear into his hairline. "Bah, since when? Ye are both just like ye mother was."

Aviva let it slide; she did not have time to debate her stubborn streak. "Do you know which watch house he got taken to?"

"East side, but I don't see how that is much use."

"Why?"

"Cause with the tournament there be no officers around to go with ye to get him out or ye will have to pay."

Aviva thought of her small amount of savings hidden in her room. She would have to use it to bail him out. The only good thing out of this mess was that East side watch house was only a few streets away, so she wouldn't waste too much time getting there. "I got to go," she yelled as she ran from the stables.

As Aviva hurried from the stables she ran headlong into General Alloshenka. "Viv, shouldn't you be with housekeeper?"

"Yes, sir." She dropped her head in respect. The General was one of the few people who treated her kindly without expecting anything in return and she always tried to repay that.

"Why are you rushing out of the stables then?"

She looked into his concerned, watery green eyes that were heavily lined with wrinkles. "I don't want to get anyone in trouble but Shai got locked up last night and I am off to get him out. I thought you would want your best swordsman at the tournament today."

This brought a croaky laugh from the old man. "Oh, you are a clever girl. Appealing to my vanity."

She blinked innocently at him.

General Alloshenka turned to the younger stiff-backed man in a crisp uniform with a shiny new badge on the lapel that stood slightly behind him. "Sergeant, go with Aviva and bail out her brother. Assure the watch that he will be properly punished for whatever misdemeanor occurred."

The sergeant saluted the General and looked at Aviva, his round face expressionless. "Which watch house?"

"East side."

"Come along then." He didn't wait to see if she followed, he simply began to stride across the large marshaling area.

They didn't speak all the way there, which was absolutely fine by Aviva who felt small talk was overrated. There was only so many times you could comment on the weather. Or maybe he didn't speak to her because he thought his warrior brand was of a higher standing than her own brand. Either way, at this moment, she had enough to worry about.

The two guards left to care for the lock up while everyone else was at the tournament looked a little surly when Aviva and the Sergeant walked in. "I understand you have Shai in custody," the Sergeant said as soon as he stepped into the room.

"That's right. He was making a nuisance of himself last night."

"He will be dealt with accordingly, but at the moment he is required elsewhere."

The guard that had answered looked dubious. "I don't think he is in any condition to compete today."

"Ready or not, the General is expecting him."

"Very well. Let me get the book for you to sign the release forms."

The other guard stood and took a large set of keys from a draw. "I'll go get our guest."

Aviva stood, silently waiting and thankful that she didn't have to use her meager savings to bail her brother out. If she believed in the Gods she would say that they had perhaps helped in coincidentally running into the General at the right moment, but most of the time she struggled to think the Gods were real, as then she would have to consider them capricious and cruel for what they put people through.

Within a few minutes, the guard had returned with Shai who looked a little haggard and unkempt, but not injured. His dark brown curls were sticking out everywhere and his blue tunic had a tear along the right shoulder.

"Thanks, sis, knew I could count on you to find me and get me out," he said brightly. "Any chance you brought food with you?"

She wanted to glower at him, but his devilish attitude always won her over and she laughed beside her better judgment.

"No, there will be something at the tournament. We don't have time to dawdle here. You don't want to miss out on the qualifying rounds."

The siblings followed the Sergeant out of the watch house.

"I am heading back to the garrison. Do you two think you can get to the tournament without incident? You both seem to have a knack for not being where you are supposed to be." His tone showed how much he didn't appreciate having to bail out Shai.

Shai saluted his superior.

"Thank you for taking the time to get me out. I understand you have more important things to do."

The crisp uniformed officer nodded his head.

"Very well, be on your way. And soldier?"

"Yes?"

"Put on a good show. Let the painful prince know that we come from strong stock."

Shai nodded and Aviva hid her smile by ducking her head.

"I will do my best," he answered.

"The general is counting on it, and by the look of it so is your sister."

As soon as the Sergeant was out of sight, Aviva linked her arm through her brother's and they began to walk toward the city gates. "What happened," she asked.

"We were having a quiet round of cards when this loud-mouthed toff comes in claiming he can best us all. I told him to quieten down and put his money where his mouth was. One of his guards took exception to how I spoke and told me I needed to leave. Kept saying I didn't know who I had just insulted. Told him I didn't care and that I wasn't going anywhere until I had finished my drink."

Aviva shook her head at the audacity of whoever the toff and his over important guard was. "Probably here to compete in the tournament today."

Shai looked surprised. "I don't know, he looked like he had enough money."

"Those types never have enough money. Imagine what ten times his weight in gold and gems would be. I don't think there are many men from this area who are prepared to give that a pass because they already have money." She tugged on his arm. "So, what happened when you said you needed to finish your drink?"

"The guard got all surly and attempted to wrestle my arm behind my back. I can only assume the idea was to frog march me out of there. I declined the invitation by punching him in the face, which for some reason, the other guard got all huffy about and jumped in."

Aviva grimaced at his cavalier attitude. "They could have hurt you."

"Please, do I look hurt?"

"Well, no, but that is not the point. This is our chance to get out of here, start fresh, where no one orders us around. If you had been hurt then how could you have competed today?"

"You worry too much." Shai looked down at her, his soft brown eyes mischievous. "And besides, even when we live on the farm I have a feeling there will still be one person ordering me around."

"Oh, ha ha, you are so funny."

They reached the main town gate and stopped their sibling bickering as the chaotic scene engulfed them. "Where did all these people come from?" she asked.

People were setting up makeshift market stalls any-where the whim took them, in turn creating bottlenecks as people couldn't find a quick way around the soon gathering crowds, especially if there was food or alcohol being sold. Hawkers who carried trays of their wares slung around their necks called out to passersby and several bards and a traveling dancing troupe had set up a small area where they were currently giving an ener-getic performance to the encouragement of the crowd. It appeared that the town of Binttle had turned out in full and had decided a simple tournament for the prince's Champion would be a fabulous excuse to let their hair down.

"It looks like every townsperson and outlying farmer are here to compete or celebrate," commented Shai.

Aviva looked around. "Any idea where we should be going?" she called out over the merriment surrounding them.

"My guess is to that tent." Shai pointed to his left.

Aviva followed the direction he indicated and saw a wooden structure with what looked like a tent awning over it.

"Good guess," she agreed. "Lead the way."

Not wanting to be separated from her brother but knowing it would be stupid to try to walk arm in arm with him through this congested space, she let go of his arm and just like when she was a child she stepped behind him and took hold of the back of his coat.

"Aw, Viv," he said as he looked back over his shoulder.

"No time for sentimentality, we are running late."

Aviva held tight to him as they moved through the crowd. Memories of her following him everywhere like this when they were little flooded her thoughts. Her protector. Shai was eight years older than Viv and had always taken the role of protector seriously. It had been a cute little thing between them as children, but when they had become orphans, he had taken the role to heart, and she loved him even more for it. But of late, it felt more like she was protecting him than he her.

In a shorter time than Aviva thought possible they arrived at what started to look like a far more organized area. Drill Sergeant Fabbron was in his element; directing the crowds to move along and find a place around the viewing circles that had been assigned to accommodate so many candidates. A large tent with soldiers in the uniform of the prince stood in the entrance with a scribe standing to the side, taking notes as they allowed what looked to be competitors through.

As they got closer, Shai swore and Aviva looked around his back to see a soldier scowling at him. The soldier had a swollen black eye. Aviva groaned.

Chapter 7

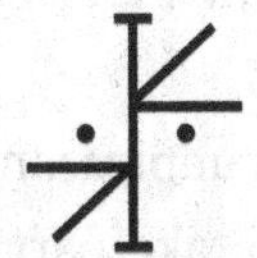

Tommofey

P rince Tommofey was feeling poorly. He had drunk far too much of the swill that passed as mead in this backward town the night before and was paying for it today. His palate was far more accustomed to a fine wine from the cooler regions, but the barrel he had brought from home had run out a month ago, and he hadn't managed to find a decent red since. He had drunk enough mead that taste didn't matter as much.

Tommofey had not slept well as he had dreamt of his oldest brother standing over him, a blood-soaked sword swinging down towards his neck. It had been startling in its clarity and it had taken him well over a turning to fall back to sleep. Just as he had managed to fall back to sleep, Tom woke, shaking from another dream. This time he had dreamed their positions reversed; Tommofey was now standing over the vanquished Harlonngraith, and Lady Darria cheered in the background. He felt sickened by the look of victory in her eyes as she watched him raise the bloody sword. Tommofey had not slept after that; instead, he had chosen to sit by the open window and listen to the sound of the waves crashing below. Attempting to distract himself from his misgivings about his mother, he had lit several lanterns and spent the next few turnings before dawn arrived making notes in his journal.

The sky was again its unpleasant grey, and the crowds that had turned out to take part in the tournament to be his Champion was heartening. The maps all said that Binttle was a large town, but Tom was starting to think if he looked at the town statistics it could possibly be reclassified into a small city. The garrison here and in Pluddgish had created far more industry, and the population had grown once soldiers retired and started families. None of this had been originally planned for. These were things that fascinated Tom. With the right planning, Binttle had the potential to be so much more.

The cheering of the crowds brought his focus back to the now and he recrossed his legs in an attempt to find a more comfortable position. Four sparring circles had been roped off and a platform built in the center of the circles which gave him the ability to face any circle he chose. The many areas operating at once meant they could cycle through the competitors quickly, with each area being set up for the next fight while one was in progress.

The rules were simple. You could use whatever weapon you chose and you won by either touching your opponent three times with your weapon, or if your opponent yielded. There had been some discussion about letting the fighters have no weapons and just use their knuckles, but it was pointed out quickly that their ultimate opponent was no doubt skilled, so a thug would not be enough.

Privately, Tommofey was relieved. The idea of a blood-bath was not his idea of entertainment. He could appreciate a fine swordsman, especially after traveling with his men and watching them spar together once camp was set up. Two men just hitting each other as hard as they could held no appeal.

The morning had been spent watching what were clearly farmhands, guildsmen, and other Common brand wearing citizens whack each other with swords. There had been several unfortunate incidents through sheer stupidity when two unskilled people were put against each other and the garrison chirurgeon and the three town chirurgeons spent the morning sewing up the local idiots whose thoughts of gold outweighed their common sense.

There had been moments of an interesting battle when a garrison soldier had come up against one of the few guards that were part of the prince's entourage who had volunteered to help find the Champion. But those had been rare moments.

Tommofey lifted his hand and Griggory came to stand beside him, a jug in his hand ready to pour him the cider he had been sipping on. "No," Tommofey spoke above the cheering and jeering of the crowd. "I think I will break my fast now. Inform Captain Albertinne I want the tent cleared."

The skinny Page scurried down the few steps of the platform to one of the guards below where he spoke quickly. The guard nodded and then spoke to another guard who moved off into the crowd. The first guard then quickly issued more instructions and within a very short time, Tommofey found himself standing in the middle of the guard formation walking to the large tent that was being used as a gathering entry point for the competitors as well as a resting place if the prince required.

His head was pounding by the time they reached the tent and he was clammy from the heat of the morning as well as the cloak he had chosen to wear in an attempt to keep the dust from the dry grassland from his clothing. The tent was stuffy and Tommofey contained his groan of dissatisfaction until he had been ushered into the private area behind a large hanging curtain on one side of the tent where there was a cot, table, and chair set up. As well as a basin, ewer, and cloth which he went to immediately after divesting himself of his heavy cloak.

The prince let his shoulder's sag and his worry showed as he again questioned his sanity in following the words of the Seer. The cool water on his face did help to freshen his outlook as well as cool him. Tommofey sat on the folding chair, and Griggory was quick to uncover the tray to reveal a selection of cold meats, slices of cheese, and a half loaf of bread. Taking his time, he nibbled on a slice of cheese, enjoying the tangy flavor. Within a quarter turning he was feeling more like himself and almost ready to go out and see how the tournament was progressing. Surely they had managed to complete the first two rounds by now and would be rid of most of the riff raff.

"Griggory, find me Captain Albertinne."

"Yes, Your Highness." The boy bowed and scurried out of the tent area.

His Page returned shortly with the captain in tow. "Your Highness sent for me?" Albertinne asked as he entered.

"Yes, Captain. Report on today's proceedings."

"The second round is done and all of the untrained idiots and those with far lesser skills have been eliminated. By my calculations, there are possibly one hundred candidates left, and from what I can see about three showing what you are really looking for. But until we reach the final rounds there may be someone conserving their energy and not ready to reveal themselves yet."

Tommofey nodded. "Very well, I shall be out shortly." It was clearly a dismissal and the captain took it that way, saluting smartly and leaving.

Looking at the heavy cloak that lay across the cot, Tommofey decided that if was going to wear it to keep his clothes clean he would do it without wearing his vest and coat. He would just wear his shirt as the day had become hotter than he thought it would. The continually overcast sky belied the heat in the air.

After rearranging his clothing, Tom knew he couldn't put it off any longer and after relieving himself in the pot, he pushed aside the curtain and went to make his way back to the platform to watch the ongoing tournament to find him a Champion to win him the throne of Segarris. A group of people standing at the opposite opening caught his attention and his eyes lingered on the woman standing amongst them. She was beautiful, with gorgeous long caramel colored curls under a lavender bonnet, and he wondered why he thought he knew her. Something was said and her eyes flashed angrily, and immediately Tom-mofey recalled who she was. She was the insolent woman in the stables who had thrown a horse blanket at him and told him to saddle his own horse. What was she doing here?

Aviva

"I think you neglected to tell me something," Aviva accused Shai under her breath as she watched the prince stalk in their direction.

"Really?" he asked, his face giving away what he thought to be a marvelous joke.

"Uh, that the prince was the toff you had words with last night."

"His gold is good, so what does it matter? Let me fight and prove I'm the best and get this farm for you."

"No, it's okay. I have changed my mind. We can do it without him."

"No, we can't," answered Shai.

Aviva could feel the prince's contempt from here. The last time she had seen him she had thrown a saddle blanket at him. Though, in her defense, she had no idea who he was at the time, but underneath it all she prob-ably still would have done it anyway. She didn't like rude and entitled people regardless of their brand in life. She tugged on the back of Shai's coat that she still held tightly.

"No, seriously, let's go. I have saved almost two thirds of my half, it won't take more than a year or two to get the rest," she hissed into his ear.

Shai threw her a strange look. "What's with you?"

"And what is going on here?" interrupted the prince as he approached.

The soldier with the black eye answered. "Your Highness, this is the man who was insolent to you last night."

"Ah, I see."

Shai bowed deeply. "I am Shai, this is my sister Aviva."

"So, you both have an issue with authority," the prince said with a distasteful look that Aviva wanted to wipe from his face.

"We have no issue with authority, but most assuredly with boys who have not been taught better manners by their mothers." She glared at him.

"I take it you have met my sister then?" Shai interjected with a cheeky grin.

Tommofey ignored the question and looked down at Shai. "What are you doing here? I am required at the tournament."

"I am here to compete in your tournament."

The guard with the black eye scoffed. "You?"

Shai shrugged. "Why not?"

"The first rounds are already completed."

Aviva's emotions were all over the place as she listened to the exchange. On one hand there was nothing more she wanted than to show this rude guard as well as the pompous prince exactly how amazing her brother was, but she also didn't want to have to spend more time than absolutely necessary around the obnoxious man.

She tugged again on her brother's jacket. "Come on, it's not worth it."

Shai turned around and faced Aviva, he held both her hands in his and squeezed gently. It wasn't until that moment did she see him for what he had become since returning. How had she missed it? Shai's brown eyes were drawn and puffy, the undertone of his skin more yellow. His skin looked drier and taught, yet swollen. Aviva had been surrounded by men all her life and she had seen too many soldiers drink themselves to death. Shai was showing some of the typical outward signs of over drinking.

"I am truly sorry, Viv, but this is the only way," he spoke quietly to her.

"What do you mean?"

"You have done brilliantly, but I am useless. My money is gone. Our money is gone."

Aviva closed her eyes against his words. All her hard work, her skimping and saving, was for naught.

"Viv, look at me," he pleaded. "I am sorry, but this is how I can make it up to you." Shai squeezed her hands tighter. "Trust me, it will all work out."

She opened her eyes to stare at him. She wanted to yell and scream and shout at him how mean and selfish and awful he was, but she didn't. This was Shai, the only person in the world who cared if she lived or died, who thought of her with fondness and not harsh words.

"I trust you," was all she said.

"Good." He grinned at her and winked before he turned back to the tall prince. "Just to be clear, what am I getting myself in for? What is the reward?"

Surprisingly the prince answered. "Ten times your weight in gold and gems."

"And what do I have to do to claim it?"

"After you are the successful candidate here you then will travel with me to the Arena where you will enter as my Champion and fight my brother's Champion. You must win that battle to claim your riches."

"And what do you get out of this?"

Prince Tommofey looked appalled at the question as if Shai were an idiot. "I get to be king."

Aviva looked up at him, at his arrogant demeanor, and wondered if she really wanted her brother to fight for this man, to make him king? He was self-indulgent and rude, neither a good quality for a king. What had seemed like a perfect solution to their money problems was no longer so appealing.

Chapter 8

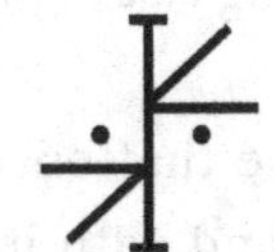

Tommofey

The exchange between the siblings had brought an unexpected lump to Tommofey's throat. The closeness displayed had been something he had always longed for, but of course never got to experience. The prince wondered if his half-brothers, Harlonngraith and Platisse, were this close.

"Your Highness, do you really think this is a good idea?" the black eyed guard questioned.

"Why not? He bested you and another last night with little effort, and he was well into his cups by that point. I am looking for my Champion and I will not leave any stone unturned." Tommofey shrugged as he turned away. "And if he isn't as good as he claims then you get to watch him be brought down a peg or two for his hubris."

Shai coughed loudly, Tommofey barely refrained from rolling his eyes as he turned back. "Yes?"

"Thank you," the young man said, all of his earlier bravado gone. "But there is one minor issue."

"Yes?" Tommofey gritted his teeth. What was it with people expecting him to do things for them?

"I am a swordsman." Shai spread his arms wide.

"And?"

"Well, my sword is back at the garrison. I didn't take it out when I went drinking last night."

"You are a warrior?"

Shai lifted the sleeve that covered his left wrist to reveal the Warrior brand with its horizontal line and inverted V on the underside of the line, and a dot in the V's center. "I served under your father for two years."

The mix of emotions that flooded Tommofey at those words was unexpected and confusing. He couldn't even label most of them. "Mmmm...that will get you no favors." His eyes flicked to the man's sister, for once silent, standing behind her brother. She looked concerned, but he doubted it was for him. No one cared about him, other than what he could give them. Tommofey wondered if she had ever met his father. What did it matter? He told himself, *you are here because of him and the mess he left.* "I am certain one of your fellow soldiers can lend you one of their swords."

"But..." the woman interrupted.

"Do you not have somewhere to be other than here pestering me?" He watched her eyes widen as if she recalled something.

Satisfied with the outcome and pleased to simply get away from the obnoxious woman, Tommofey waited for his bodyguards to form around him and they headed back out the other side of the tent and toward the platform. As he settled into his chair, his thoughts skimmed over the conversation and for the first time since they had arrived did he fully appreciate that there were many people in this town who had possibly spent time with his father and could tell Tommofey more about him. After all, Binttle was where he had been based from when he wasn't fighting skirmishes on Pluddgish. Then again, a bitter internal voice whispered, *why bother, when he didn't care about you?* Before he could spiral, Tommofey pushed aside those thoughts and brought his mind back to the thing that mattered now. His Champion.

The next two rounds of the tournament went far quicker as the sheer volume of participants had finally been eroded into a manageable size. The final battle of the fourth round was about to begin and Tommofey drained his cider and beckoned for another as Shai walked into the center of the allocated sparring circle. Having missed the first two rounds, this would be only the second time Tommofey watched him fight. The first had been totally uninspiring as his opponent had tripped on his sword and fallen flat on his face. The young man had squealed that he yielded when Shai had held the sharp blade of his borrowed sword against his opponent's throat.

A woman about the same height as Shai, approximately six foot two inches tall, stepped into the circle. She carried a thick chain that looked to hold a circular disc at one end. The disc was hollow in the center and had several nasty looking spikes on its outer edge. Tommofey felt a little ill as he looked at the weapon. His overactive imagination was giving him ideas of all the nasty things she could do with that.

Shai bowed mockingly to the tall woman who did nothing but stand there and stare at him.

"Excuse me, Your Highness." Griggory spoke quietly. "Captain Albertinne and General Alloshenk seek permission to sit with you and provide you with information of the final fighters, if you so wish?"

"That would be welcome, as long as they don't have the mayor with them." Tommofey stood and allowed his seat to be moved to accommodate two more chairs. An oblong table was also brought up and placed in front of the chairs—Tommofey wondered why that hadn't been done before. Now he had somewhere to rest his drink.

"Your lunch will be served shortly," one of the men that had brought the table bowed to the prince.

It was only when they were all seated and facing the two circles on one side of the platform did Tommofey realize that the fight had already begun. The crowd *oohed* and *aahed* as the female fighter held up her strange weapon and stopped Shai's overhead swing. As the sword blades slid along the outer edge of the circular weapon, it must have hit one of the spikes as the warrior flicked her wrist forcing Shai to step back and reset.

"What type of weapon is that?" asked the prince.

"It's a Shacram; quite common amongst the locals on the Lobbregath Islands," answered General Alloshenka. "Shai has been sparring against that weapon and that particular soldier for years. It's impressive if you don't know what you are doing, but a skilled swordsman like Shai will counteract it effectively."

"Is he that good?" asked Albertinne.

"Yes."

"There is something about his style..." The Captain's voice trailed off as he watched the warrior.

Tommofey was only half listening to the men; he was too busy watching with fascination as the woman lengthened the chain and began to spin the lethal disc over her head. The crowd took a step back as she brought it down lower with a flick of her wrist. As the weapon swung towards Shai's feet, he planted his sword tip in the earth and jumped backward. The weapon missed him and the chain quickly wound around the blade. The sudden loss of momentum of the chain pulled the woman forward and she stumbled for a brief moment, but it was enough. Shai bent down and took up the chain giving it a solid tug causing the woman to lose her balance completely. He was on her immediately and to everyone's surprise drew a short knife from his boot and held it high as if he was going to plunge it into her chest. "Yield?" he shouted.

"What is he doing?" asked Tommofey.

"Being dramatic. His sister is even worse," the general answered.

"I have had the displeasure of meeting his sister." Tommofey shuddered and pulled a face. Both men laughed. "Twice."

"My commiserations," General Alloshenk commented. "She is dramatic and headstrong, not an ideal combination in a woman."

"Thankfully, I am looking for my Champion not my queen."

"Is she beautiful?" asked Albertinne.

Tommofey surprised himself with answering. "Very."

"A beautiful, headstrong, dramatic woman sounds like someone who would make your life more interesting, in my opinion."

"I have my mother for that. I want quiet, pliable, and not prone to seeing shadows in every corner." Tommofey watched as the woman nodded and held up her hands in supplication.

Shai reversed the knife and tucked it inside his boot before he held out his hand and helped the woman up. "And there goes the final female competitor," announced the Captain.

"I know there are women walking around with the warrior brand, but did you expect one to be good enough to be my Champion?" Tommofey raised his eyebrows.

"I don't think the army could produce one," was the response. It was an odd answer but Tommofey didn't care enough to follow it up. They were now down to the final eight and that was far more important.

Shai walked over to the sword still sticking out of the earth with the weapon wrapped around it. He took hold of the handle and pulled it out of the ground, brandishing it high like a conquering hero. The crowd responded with good natured cheering. Shai didn't move out of the circle, rather he simply took the jug of water offered to him by another soldier and had several swigs before handing it back.

Tommofey's eyes wandered over the crowd as he waited for the scribe assigned to keep track of the men to allocate the next fighters. He looked at these people who would be his to rule and all he felt was empty. Nothing stirred within him or told him that other than fulfilling the wishes of his mother choosing to fight for the throne had been the right decision. People weren't hanging around the bottom of the platform trying to garner his attention, to beg for favors, or even bother to denounce him. Contrary to his mother's opinion, it seemed the world did not care if he sat on the throne or not.

A shorter man entered the roped off area of the fighting circle and clasped Shai's arm in greeting. It looked like Shai would be the first to fight in this round. They both drew their swords and the sound of metal rang out across the hushed crowd as their weapons clashed. The first few blows were fast as the shorter man rushed at Shai, making him step back. Not close enough to accidentally step on the rope and disqualify himself but enough for the crowd to begin to chatter.

Several men and women swarmed up the stairs of the platform and began to place large trays of food on the table. They did it with a minimum fuss, but Tommofey on several occasions had to lean from side to side to see what was happening below. One of the serving girls placed something and turned to leave but stopped, her back to him, blocking his entire view. "Move," he bellowed at her. This made her turn. Tommofey groaned inwardly—it was the sister. He couldn't remember her name.

She glared at him but said nothing; he didn't look away. It was only the yell of the crowd that broke the stalemate. Tommofey stood to look over the top of her as she spun back to watch her brother take a step back to allow the shorter man the chance to retrieve the sword he had just dropped. "How many is that?" Tom asked the men seated beside him.

"Two," answered the captain.

The girl didn't move and Tommofey remained standing as they watched Shai swing his sword in a fancy circle on either side of his body for several seconds before engaging with his opponent. "He really is cocky," commented the prince.

"Ha," was the rejoinder from his sister.

In a few rapid moves it was all over. The shorter man now had a shallow gash across his left cheek which was slowly bleeding.

The girl went to walk down the stairs when the general stopped her. "Aviva, stay and serve us."

"Yes, sir," she answered with more respect in her voice than Tommofey had heard before. She turned and walked back up the stairs and came to stand beside the old man and picked up his plate and a large serving fork. "What would you like to eat?"

The general smiled at the young woman and gave her clear instructions to what he wanted. She complied without complaint.

Prince Tommofey watched Aviva select several thin slices of the deliciously smelling roast boar on the platter. She also piled on sprouts, small tubers, carrots, and a thick slice of bread. With a practiced flourish she drizzled gravy over the meat and then set it down in front of the general.

There was no wasting of time and the next battle had already begun and the crowds were cheering, but Tommofey continued to watch the woman. He guessed she was a few years older than him. She turned to captain Albertinne. "Sir, may I serve you?" she asked and pointed to his plate.

"Yes, please. The same as the general will be fine." Aviva began to pile the succulent boar onto Albertinne's plate. "Your brother is doing well."

Captain Albertinne making conversation with the woman was a surprise and Tommofey was a little put out with the whole situation. Did they all forget he was the one with the title? He sat there, his lips compressed in anger as she finished serving before turning to him. "Sir, may I serve you?"

"It's *Your Highness*, or *My Lord*, and I should have been served first."

Aviva curtsied deeply and slowly, it was clear she was mocking him. "I apologize profusely for thinking, Your Highness, being a fit and young man, would willingly allow two men who serve your country and are your elders to have their meals served before your own."

He ground his teeth in an effort to not retaliate with harsh words. She thought she was clever? Well, two could play at this game, and he had no intention of using his title to have her punished. He would much rather bide his time and bring her down a peg or two with his own wit. "Griggory will serve me."

"Very well, My Lord." She stepped away from him and moved to stand slightly to the side and back of General Alloshenka.

By the time Griggory had finished putting a plate together for the prince and had stepped out of the way, the last of the battles for the round was coming to its conclusion. There were now only four people left in the tournament. Tommofey looked at the men who were now being herded to stand at the foot of the platform. One of these four, according to the Seer, was to be his Champion.

"May I say a few words to the men?" Captain Albertinne asked Tommofey.

"Certainly," he agreed, secretly pleased he didn't need to say anything to the warriors standing before him. Public speaking was something he didn't feel comfortable with, and honestly, he wouldn't know what to say.

"Soldiers, you have done exceedingly well in reaching this stage and I congratulate you. However, this is not the time for heroes or show-offs. The prince is here to find his Champion and you will be required to fight in six weeks. Which means that we cannot afford to have any accidental injuries as there may not be time to recover." He paused and stared down at each of them in turn. "Do I make myself clear?"

In unison all four men answered, "Yes, sir."

Captain Albertinne returned to his seat and the first two men were taken to the fighting circle. "Begin," called Tommofey as the crowd turned to him. The two men, both local soldiers from the area, were excellent swordsmen and both managed to score a hit on their opponent. They were masterful with their blocks, parries, and overhead strokes, and it was clear these two were used to sparring together as they anticipated each other's moves. The ebb and flow of the battle was exciting and the crowd roared their appreciation when one of the men tapped his blade on the shoulder of his opponent. One more hit and they would have the first to go through to the final round.

Back and forth they stalked, at times circling around each other before one would pounce in a flurry of moves. Unexpectedly, the man with the one-point advantage changed direction mid step and switched hands, suddenly coming at his opponent from the opposite angle and catching him off guard enough to score the final hit on his thigh.

There was loud applause and cheering as they clasped forearms and the victor returned to the base of the platform while the loser was led away.

Shai and his opponent, a soldier from Tommofey's own personal guard, were led to the same circle that had just been vacated. The prince sat forward in his chair, for reasons he couldn't understand, he was a little more invested in the outcome of this fight. "Begin," he ordered.

"This will be the real test," the general said to no one in particular.

"What makes you say that?" asked Captain Albertinne.

"Trosswil, the one that just won, has never managed to score a single point upon Shai when they spar, regardless of weapon or just bare knuckles. Shai has the ability to get under his skin and Trosswil loses all focus," General Alloshenka explained. He turned to the captain. "Your man there seems to know exactly what he is doing and has been conserving himself as much as possible, so I think this will be Shai's true test."

"Lieutenant Pynnan is the best our army has to offer from the twin cities. He has done as well as what I thought he would," Captain Albertinne said proudly.

This made Tommofey frown. "If he is that good, why are we here? Why did I put myself through the months of travel when my Champion was in my guard the entire time?"

"Because Shai will beat Pynnan and then Trosswil and be your Champion," a confident female voice piped up causing Tommofey to grimace. He had forgotten she was still around. He did not take his eyes off the two men currently duelling for the right to fight to the death for him.

"Did you not just hear the captain?" the prince demanded.

"I heard."

Tommofey almost cheered with the rest of the gathered crowd when the Lieutenant's flat side of his sword grazed along Shai's upper arm. His want to turn and side eye Aviva at this moment was so strong he almost gave in to the childish whim, but all too quickly his thoughts went back to the epic battle in front of them. Shai and Pynnan parried back and forth, both impressive with their skills. They appeared evenly matched and when it was the flat of Shai's blade that connected with Pynnan's calf, Tommofey could no longer keep denying the man's skill.

The two men circled each other and at one point they both smiled, clearly enjoying battling a man who challenged them. Their powerful blows against each other's long swords rebounded out across the field. It was as if everyone held their collective breath. This was turning into a battle that would be talked about for years to come.

Tommofey had never taken much notice of his soldiers and their abilities other than to rely on the fact they were capable of protecting him and willing to die for his continued safety. But this was exhilarating.

Pynnan launched into an attack with several blows that would have maimed Shai if they had connected. Shai cleverly spun out of the way and waggled a finger at him as if he were a naughty boy. The crowd cheered and laughed, but from the platform there was a low rumble of dissatisfaction that seemed to be emanating from the captain.

"Problem?" asked Tommofey.

"He just went against a direct order." Captain Albertinne answered.

"Shai has that effect on people," General Alloshenka commented.

"Is he a troublemaker?" the prince asked. "I don't need someone who will cause issues. This is far too important an outcome."

"If it's that important, why leave it up to chance then?" Alloshenka asked.

"It was not chance. I do not risk my ascension to the throne on chance." He sat a little straighter in his chair. "As I explained in my original missive, I am here on the guidance of the Seer. She, however, didn't bother to tell me how to find my Champion, just where. The tournament and outrageous reward seemed like the most effective way to uncover the best fighter in the area."

The old soldier nodded at him. "Makes more sense to why you would hold a tournament here than simply march in here and demand the best soldier. The Gods are playing, and everyone must earn their place at the table."

"I couldn't presume the Champion would be a soldier, all I knew is that I would find them here."

As they spoke, the two men in the fighting circle continued to trade strikes before retreating and then feinting and trading a few more blows. They had fallen into an almost hypnotic rhythm.

"Oh, he is clever," Captain Albertinne commented. Before Tommofey could even ask, Albertinne went on. "Shai is drawing him out of the center. Pynnan thinks he is winning as Shai is slowly appearing to retreat, but what he's doing is bringing them both to the edge without Pynnan taking notice."

As the captain pointed out what was happening, Shai slowly began to position himself with his back to the center of the inner circle, while Pynnan now had his back to the rope that defined the edge. He could no longer see how close he was. Shai and Pynnan continued to swing at each other when Shai suddenly grinned and ran at the lieutenant, his sword raised. By instinct, Pynnan took two steps back and Shai stopped running. "Two," he called out as he gestured to the man's foot that now rested on the rope.

Shai sauntered back to the middle and waited for Pynnan to join him. It was now two to one in Shai's favor.

Tommofey watched with growing appreciation at the ease in which Shai attacked Pynnan as soon as he returned to the center, he was giving him no time to reset. He looked like a warrior now, his face clear with his intention. Shai was here to win. His sword swung low as he pushed his advantage, and then just as quickly, he stepped back which forced the lieutenant to overreach. Surprisingly, Shai dropped his sword and reached out with both hands and took the wrist of Pynnan while stepping back in closer but turning his body to face away, pushing out his hip and before anyone could guess what would happen, the heavy set lieutenant was lifted off the ground and spun over the body of Shai, landing flat on his back. Pynnan's sword now rested in Shai's hand and he gently lowered it to touch his opponent's chest.

"That was quite a move," Captain Albertinne said as he stood and joined in the spontaneous applause that followed.

"Shai and Aviva lived on the Pluddgish for many years when they were younger. Their father was the swordsmith assigned to the garrison there. The soldiers used to play with the children and Shai loved to spar with them. When they were brought here to live when the island was deemed too dangerous by your father, the soldiers allowed him to practice with them whenever he was allowed. Even before he was branded Shai was better than most," General Alloshenka explained proudly.

Tommofey listened without comment as the older men talked.

"And where did he pick up that move, do you know? It's something similar to what we teach now, but it has been modified," Albertinne asked.

General Alloshenka shrugged his frail shoulders. "I cannot say."

"The king," Aviva's voice spoke over the General's.

"I beg your pardon?" Tommofey said, turning to look at her.

"The king. He learned it from your father."

Chapter 9

Aviva

Aviva felt like singing but didn't. Instead, she hummed to herself. Humming didn't draw attention, singing loudly usually did. Her brother had been magnificent and the final round had gone exactly as General Alloshenka had warned the prince it would. Trosswil had not managed to get near Shai, and rather than drag it out, Shai had tapped the soldier with his sword three times in quick succession. It had been anti-climactic after the masterful battle between Shai and the lieutenant prior. But now it was done. Shai was proclaimed Champion for Prince Tommofey and they were one fight away from having enough money to do whatever they wanted. Even the fact she would have to spend the next six weeks with the obnoxious prig of a prince could not dampen Aviva's mood as she hummed loudly.

The morning had dawned, and for once, Aviva had gone about her tasks without fuss. As she completed each job, she said a silent goodbye to the person she worked with and moved on to the next. The morning had passed quickly and once she had said goodbye to the horses still in the stable, she had hurried up to her room to start packing. Which was where the housekeeper found her a half turning later.

"And where exactly do ye think ye going?" Housekeeper Ottilie asked from the doorway.

Aviva looked up from the clothes she had spread over the bed. It wasn't many, she didn't have an extensive wardrobe, but it was all her possessions, and she would not be leaving any behind. When her brother won the Right to Rule Challenge for the prince, Aviva was certain there would be suitable accommodation for them to stay at while they searched for their perfect home.

"Where do you think I am going?" Aviva asked, unsure what the housekeeper meant.

"Well, ye ain't going with ye brother, if that's what ye think is happening."

"And why not?"

"Did the priests change the rules while I wasn't looking, or has someone transferred ye to the prince's keeping?" Housekeeper Ottilie sounded exasperated, as if Aviva should not need explaining to.

Finally, what the housekeeper was implying dawned on Aviva, and she sank down on the bed, not caring if she wrinkled all of the clothing; after all, she would not be going anywhere.

Oh, how she hated the Gods sometimes. Or was it the priests, or maybe she should rail at the prince for enforcing the stupid law? Her feelings of loathing changed focus depending on who was telling her no. Aviva chafed at the invisible collar that held her in this place. She was owned by the garrison to serve in any capacity they saw fit, though never in an intimate way. That was frowned upon, though she wasn't sure if that role was forced upon her would anyone other than her brother interfere? After all, her brand made her meaningless, one of the unseen. It gave everyone a false sense of protection and caring for those less fortunate when in reality the Servants were little more than slaves. She was not allowed to pursue her hopes, dreams, or goals. Ever. Her servitude was unending.

"Ye have a quarter turning to tidy this up and I expect ye back in the kitchens; we have a meal to prepare."

Aviva nodded; her usual sass gone for the moment.

Housekeeper Ottilie sighed and reached out to pat the young woman on the head. "Things would go much easier for ye if ye stopped all the nonsense with the dreaming. Ye are protected here, and allowed ye freedom to be in the stables whenever there is time. Ye have been taught to read and count and are fed and clothed well. My goodness girl, even ye sass is allowed."

"You are right." Her voice was brittle. Aviva just wanted the housekeeper to leave.

"Perhaps if ye looked at finding a nice fella and concentrated on having a few bairns then ye wouldn't want for more."

Aviva shuddered deliberately. "I could think of nothing worse than tying myself to a man."

"Suit ye self." Housekeeper Ottilie shrugged. "A quarter turning to sulk is all ye going to get." With that, she spun and walked out the room, closing the door behind her, allowing Aviva some privacy to do exactly that—sulk.

Aviva sat on the bed for several minutes, glaring at her left wrist though it was covered—she always covered her brand—and wished her life was different. She imagined a life of traveling and exploring. Making her own decisions and never being told what to do. Tending and breeding the beautiful horses she loved and giving her brother a chance to rest from the years of serving on Pluddgish. Waking up when she wished, eating when she wished and what she wished, and never having to take orders. Aviva wondered if that was why the prince irritated her so much. He had everything and he behaved appallingly. He could do whatever he chose. Eating the finest foods, wearing the finest clothing. A life of indulgence and whim where his every want was answered.

It was more than the prince though. Aviva was angry at the world. Her brand was never supposed to be a Servant. There had never been a Servant in her family. But it had been commented on more than once that there were more and more Warriors and Servants coming from the Branding ceremonies over the last decade than ever before.

Slowly she stood, resigned to the fact that she was going to have to be away from her brother for many more weeks while he rode to the Arena, fought, and then returned. "You are being dramatic," she told herself as she wiped her eyes, ridding herself of the single tear that threatened to fall. She hated to cry, it made her vulnerable.

There was a tap on the door. "Viv?" her brother called.

"What?"

He opened the door and frowned as he took in her appearance and the now rumpled clothes. "You almost ready?"

"No," Aviva muttered and sagged back down on the bed.

"Well, hurry it up. The prince was very clear about how far we have to travel and how little time we have."

"I'm not going."

He looked pointedly to the clothes on her bed. "That would say otherwise."

"I can't go," she amended.

"Oh, yes, now that makes more sense," Shai answered sarcastically. "Any chance we can stop with the cryptic talk?"

"The housekeeper just pointed out I can't go with you."

He snorted at that. "And why not?"

"Because of this," Aviva yelled at him in frustration, wrenching up her sleeve to reveal the horrid Servant brand that she was convinced should never have been there.

Tommofey

The view still surprised Tommofey. Approaching Binttle from the road had been uninspiring in its blandness. All gray stone, dull and squat buildings. But from this room on the second floor of the inn that sat on the other side of the town well away from the expanse of boring browned grass was a vista of sublime beauty. An open expanse of rolling aquamarine waves, where seagulls frolicked, and several islands could be spotted on the horizon. The sea breeze brought in the smell of freedom and hope in Tommofey's mind and he had kept the windows wide open noon and night, regardless of how low the temperature dropped, though this time of year it was pleasantly comfortable.

The tournament was over, his Champion found, and they would be leaving straight after the visit from the tailor. Tommofey had made the most of delaying the tournament by two days whilst the area was prepared and had had a tailor take in his clothing as well as purchasing several pieces that would replace the too worn riding pants. He had also made certain that his warriors all received new uniforms. When they arrived at the Arena, they would arrive in the best possible condition, looking fresh and ready to lead a nation.

There was a polite knock on the door. Tommofey nodded to Griggory to let them in. He was surprised to see Shai walk in rather than the tailor.

"My Lord, I apologize for the intrusion." The soldier who was now his Champion bowed from just inside the door.

"No, it's fine. Come in." He indicated for Griggory to close the door. "I thought I would be seeing you when I paid my final respects to the general, just before we are scheduled to leave."

"I have come to negotiate my contract," Shai stated boldly.

"I beg your pardon. The terms were clear when you entered the tournament. You even questioned them, if I recall?"

"Well, I want to make an addition."

"And if I deny the request?"

Shai shrugged. "Then I won't fight for you. You can find yourself another Champion."

"You can't do that. We have an agreement." Tommofey was astounded at the audacity of the warrior. He had not expected this from the man.

"When were you planning on telling me the whole truth?" Shai moved to stand by the open window.

"What whole truth?" Tommofey asked, though he had a feeling he knew what the man was alluding to.

"Well, it seems you neglected to inform everyone that this coming battle for the throne is to the death." Shai turned to face the window. "My death," he added in a quieter voice.

The prince moved to stand beside him. "It will be my death too." They stood like that for several moments, watching the waves roll in. "You lose, we both die," he said the words softly, as if trying to manage the heaviness of them.

"I want my sister there. If these are going to be the last few weeks of my life, I want to spend them with the only family I have."

"And there will be no more changes to the terms if I agree to this?"

"No."

Tommofey held out his hand and Shai clasped his wrist. "A little less talk about it being the last weeks of our lives would be appreciated," The prince pointed out.

Shai laughed. "I have no intention of losing."

Chapter 10

Aviva

Housekeeper Ottilie stood there expecting an answer for what she thought was clearly good news she had just delivered. "Girl, don't just stand there. Get ye belongings packed. Ye are expected in the stables in a quarter turning."

Aviva took the words in and turned them over in her mind several times before it all finally registered. "I am being re-assigned to the prince's personal guard? What could they possibly want with me?" she asked.

"Didn't ask; ye don't look a gift horse in the mouth."

A soldier in his smart uniform that held the colors on his sleeve that told her he was from Prince Tommofey's men stood behind the housekeeper. Aviva guessed he was the one who had delivered the supposedly good news. While taking note of the older man, Aviva suddenly recalled stories that she had overheard some of the soldiers trade over their meals. The bragging of which camp follower was going with them on their tour came to mind and Aviva felt sick. She would not do that, not ever. Who did the prince think he was believing she would do this?

Did Shai know what was happening? Aviva doubted it; he would never put her in this position.

"I am not going anywhere until I know exactly what the expectations are."

The housekeeper snorted. "Prince Tommofey does not strike me as the type to be kept waitin. Do yeself a favor, Viv, and just pack ye things and get goin."

There was nothing more Aviva hated than to be told what to do. She often wondered if the Gods were truly cruel and thought it amusing to have put the Servant brand upon her when she loathed being constantly told where and what she needed to be doing. Weren't brands supposed to suit their wearer's? Or was it that the Gods didn't think her worthy of anything more? Now that thought was soul destroying, depressing.

Housekeeper Ottilie wiped her hands on the front of her apron as if cleansing them of the situation. "So be it, ye are a foolish girl. If I was ye I would have me bags packed and ready to go by the time whoever the soldier has gone to get arrives." And with those parting words and a shake of her head the frumpy woman departed, not bothering to close the bedroom door.

Aviva waited. She did not pace, though she wanted to, but the space was limited in the room with its single dresser, and a stool beside each of the three cots for the girls to use as a night table or seat. Instead of pacing, she counted the worn wood panels on the walls. This kept her focused and stopped her from exploding and running to the stable as she usually did when she was distressed.

Aviva had completed her counting and had returned to the original wall when she heard footsteps upon the steps. She didn't care who was approaching, Aviva was determined to uncover exactly what her role would be before she left the town.

The footsteps halted, and taking up the whole space of the door frame was the hulking, angry prince. He glowered at her for a moment before ducking under the low frame and coming to stand in the middle of the tiny space.

She knew she should curtsy, but all Aviva could focus on was how much space he took up in the tiny room that she shared with two other servants. His broad shoulders and chest were directly in her line of sight and she had to step back to see his face, he was so tall. Aviva knocked her shin as she clipped the side of the bed trying to create space between them. She grit her teeth, but showed no pain.

"I am told there is an issue. What exactly is your problem?"

His tone rankled her. Who did he think he was? "I have every right to ask questions and express my concerns."

She noted his clenched jaw. "Your brother has accepted my terms, and I believe I am being generous in allowing this added condition that you be brought along."

Aviva wanted to scratch his superior eyes out. "I am not a condition."

"You're a very disagreeable person, do you know that?" The prince frowned as he spoke, his forehead wrinkling in a way that Aviva found alarmingly distracting.

"So I have been told," she snapped back.

"Get your bag, get it packed. We leave in a quarter turning." He looked down at her, his hazel eyes hard and demanding.

Aviva stood tall, only coming up to his mid-chest and tilted her head back to glare at him. "You don't get to order me around."

"Actually, I do."

"My brand does not make me less than you." Her words were slow and deliberate.

"True, the laws protect you from that. However, I am a prince and if I claim to require your services on my journey, I can order it, and your contract will be given to me. And that is precisely what occurred. Your brother wouldn't leave without you, so things have been changed to accommodate that. Which means you will do exactly as you have been ordered and stop making a ridiculous scene about nothing and pack your bags."

Aviva crossed her arms and stood her ground. "No."

This made Prince Tommofey smirk, which for some reason made her feel uneasy. "No?"

"Are you deaf?" she retorted.

His face changed and he narrowed his gaze. "You are walking a fine line. I need your brother, which means I have to deal with you, but I will not tolerate your behavior. If you are not in the stables in a quarter turning with your bags packed I will have someone fetch you and carry you out where you will be tied to a horse—"

"You can't do that," Aviva yelled at him.

"Let me make this clear. I can and will do what it takes to get to the appointed place on time. As I explained before, your brother insisted you weren't left behind and that is what I agreed to. Nothing more, nothing less."

"I refuse to be a camp follower." She stood her ground, not cowed by his words. Aviva would not be used in that way. The thought of sex terrified her and she had managed to avoid it so far. A few men had shown interest in her over the years, but all she cared about were the horses. It was the act itself that was the issue. From what she saw of others relationships, men were too controlling and wanted everything done for them. She didn't want to be a servant in her private relationships so she did everything in her power to avoid them. Aviva had never met anyone she wanted to change her mind for.

The prince laughed. "My, you are a dramatic one. No one expects any such thing from you." He wrinkled his nose at her. "My guards are men of honor and are here to do a job."

Aviva felt herself flush. "Then what am I expected to do? You must have had to put down a reason for the transfer of contract."

Prince Tommofey rolled his eyes. "Are you slow, is there an issue with your learning? I will say this one more time, and then I am done with this conversation." He dragged out each word. "I am a prince. I can have any Servant I want assigned to me for no reason other than I wish it. I can have any soldier assigned to me on a whim. Do you understand what I am saying?"

"I am not an idiot; you do not need to be so condescending".

"Then stop behaving like one." He turned to leave.

"Wait, you haven't said what I will be doing for you." She didn't know why this was so important to her, but she kept pushing. He had told her she wouldn't be a camp follower so why did it matter?

He didn't bother to turn back but did pause in his exit. "You are a Servant. You will do chores."

"Such as?"

"God damn it, how would I know? Those matters are not my concern." The prince strode out the door.

"Arrogant prick," she muttered under her breath, smart enough to know that you didn't openly insult a prince, no matter your brand. Aviva stood there for several moments and an unexpected smile crossed her lips. There was something about that man that made her want to defy him just to see him lose his temper.

Chapter 11

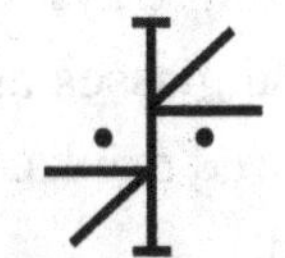

Tommofey

"Are you sure?" Tommofey asked, not hiding his annoyance.

"Yes, he's young and will bounce back, but currently your Page is far too ill to travel." The chirurgeon washed his hands in the basin that had been provided for him.

"How long?"

"At least four days."

"Impossible," Tommofey growled.

"I beg your pardon?"

"We need to be on the road by noon."

"You can be, but your Page cannot." The man spoke like Tommofey was slow in understanding.

"Fine."

There was a knock on the door that interrupted any further conversation.

"Yes?" he answered, disgruntled that he should need to do that himself.

"It's Albertinne," he announced.

"Enter."

The burly captain with his close-cropped, graying hair opened the door and continued to hold it open for the serving women who followed behind him. The two women held large serving trays. One was covered, the other contained several glasses and goblets, as well as jugs with different colored drinks. They placed the trays on the table and bowed.

The older of the two women spoke quietly. "I am told that your boy took sick in the night. Would you like one of us to stay and serve you?"

Tommofey shook his head. "I will manage."

She bowed again and they both left the room. Tommofey turned back to the doctor. "Is there anything that needs to be done for Griggory?"

"He needs to keep his fluids up and rest. A hot bath each day and steaming may help clear some of the congestion."

"It shall be seen to. Once final arrangements have been made you will be told where you shall visit him each day," explained the prince. "You are dismissed."

The man hurried from the two-bedroom suite and closed the door behind him. Tom turned to the captain who stood by the table.

"Would you care to join me in breaking my fast?" he asked.

It was not something he typically did, but Tommofey was finding not having Griggory around to be even more lonely, if possible. Sitting on the platform on the day of the tournament with Albertinne and Alloshenk had been more enjoyable than the prince wanted to admit.

"I have already broken my fast for the morning, but would be pleased to join you and have a drink while you eat."

Tommofey sat at the table and uncovered the tray laden with eggs, sausages, breads, and pastries. His mouth began to water as he piled the food onto his plate. Albertinne poured himself a juice and sat back, sipping on it. "Will the boy be okay?"

"Yes, the chirurgeon says he will be back on his feet and ready to travel in four days. Arrangements will need to be made for Griggory. See to it."

"Of course. The boy can be moved to the garrison, and I will leave one of the men with him that will escort him back to the capital once he is well. He can also make sure the doctor visits each day and that all instructions are followed. One of the men who is a father should suit the role." Albertinne drained the orange juice before going on.

Tommofey put his knife and fork down and patted his mouth with the heavy cloth napkin. The service and food at the Dancing Boar was just as good as he remembered it from on their way to Binttle. "I will also need a replacement; I cannot be expected to do without the services of a body servant for the next five weeks."

"Vetting someone at the moment may be a little tricky," admitted Albertinne.

"Mmmm." They sat in silence while Tommofey continued eating. He was annoyed with the world this morning. Why couldn't life just go to plan for more than a few days? It continuously seemed to throw obstacles in his path.

"Your Highness, I may have a solution, but you need to hear me out," Albertinne spoke into the silence.

Tom looked up from his plate suspiciously. "What did you have in mind?"

"Well…" He drew out the word. "You already have someone in your entourage that could step in."

"I do?"

"Yes, she—" Albertinne got no further.

"No," Tommofey exploded. "Absolutely not."

"But she is a Servant."

"She is also a pain in my neck."

"We don't have a lot of other choices. I am not prepared to put your safety at risk and a Page this far from the palace is almost impossible to find. Those young boys are trained early."

Tommofey closed his eyes for several moments, hoping to find another solution in the dark. What Albertinne was suggesting made sense, but he didn't have to like it.

"Fine," he eventually agreed, but held up his hand to forestall the captain in commenting. "She must be attired properly if she is to join my personal service. Her clothing has been barely acceptable for whatever she has been doing but will not be serviceable for her new role."

"Aviva has been working with the horses. Toby has taken a liking to her I am told."

"Traitorous horse," muttered Tommofey. "Have her brought here and find a seamstress. I still want to be on the road by noon."

Captain Albertinne stood and bowed. "Yes, My Lord."

As the soldier left, Tom returned to finishing his meal. He attempted not to dwell on Aviva and her soft brown eyes that appeared to take great joy in contradicting everything he said. The next five weeks now felt as if they would be even more torturous than they already were. They had one more stop at a decent-sized town and then a few smaller villages over the next two weeks, and she would need to be dressed appropriately.

After finishing his meal, Tommofey went to his desk and checked to see if the additions he had made to his map journal last night had dried enough for him to pack away his cartography set. Tom looked at the tiny details he had added that he had missed on the way to Binttle. The more accurate depiction of the road and the height of the rolling hills that surround the town.

Satisfied that it was dry, the prince took his time in placing all the items in their correct order back in the special leather case.

There was a polite tap on the door as he was buckling the straps up and grumbling under his breath at the fact he had to answer his own door. Tommofey walked over and opened it. He was greeted by a scowling Aviva.

"I was summoned." Her tone was cool.

"Did Captain Albertinne explain your new role?" he asked as she stepped into the room.

"New role?" she asked as she closed the door behind her.

Coward, he thought to himself as he turned around to face the young woman. "Yes, Griggory is unwell."

That was as far as he got. "Oh, no, where is he?"

"Resting in his room." Tom indicated the door deeper into the room.

"Poor baby." She rushed to the door.

"What are you doing?" he exclaimed.

"Checking on him. He is so far from home and is only twelve."

"You can't go in there; what happens if you get sick?"

"Bah! I'm made of sterner stuff than that."

And before he could stop her or say anything further, she opened the door and rushed in to check on his Page. Swearing under his breath, Tommofey went to follow when there was another knock on the door. Muttering that Aviva was in fact here to open doors not check on the boy, he stomped over and yanked open the door.

"Yes?"

Two women stood there, both round, one past her child bearing years, the other in the prime of them. They were both dark skinned and had long black hair that was wound up and secured on the top of their heads. The older lady's hair was streaked with gray. Tommofey guessed they were mother and daughter.

"Your highness, we are the dressmakers you asked for." The mother curtsied, quickly followed by her daughter.

"Good, come in." He stepped aside and let them into the large room. The younger lady placed a basket she was carrying onto the oblong table. "My maid is in urgent need of new clothing. I want three dresses in navy blue that can be modified for riding."

"What is going on?" Aviva asked as she walked out of the room, wiping her hand on her over apron.

"These ladies are here to dress you correctly."

"Correctly?" she asked, her voice rising an octave.

"Yes, you are to take on the responsibilities of Griggory for the next five weeks, and I can't have my Servant dressed in anything other than appropriate clothing."

"No," she responded.

"Yes," Tom insisted.

"No, you can't make me."

Prince Tommofey took a deep breath and turned to the dressmakers who were standing uncomfortably to one side. "Clearly we do not have time for you to make anything, so I am hoping you will have something in your shop that is suitable and can be altered?"

"They must be navy?" the daughter asked.

"Not completely navy, but she must look like she fits in with the entourage and colors."

"Yes, there are several things that I believe can be modified." The woman looked critically at Aviva. "It should not be too difficult."

"We leave at noon."

The younger woman took up her basket. "We will be back in two turnings with something suitable."

"You do not wish to measure her first?"

The older woman looked at Aviva warily. "Ah, no, I have been doing this long enough that I only need to measure for the finer details."

"Good." The prince nodded and saw them out. He turned back to the woman who stood there fuming. "What exactly is your problem, Aviva? Are you disagreeable for no other reason than you want to be?"

She opened her mouth and closed it before opening it again. "No."

"Then please enlighten me to your continuing foul mood."

"You can't order me to do something."

He rolled his eyes at her. "I think we established in Binttle, that as I am a prince and you are a Servant, that is exactly how our relationship works."

"You could ask instead of order."

He blinked at her, trying to understand what she meant.

"Why would I do that?"

"Because it's polite."

Tommofey laughed. "You will do it because that is what is required. Now, I want these breakfast dishes cleared, just call the housekeeper for that, and then I want my clothing packed."

Aviva stood there and glared at him a little longer. "And if I say no?"

"Do not test me. I will not tolerate that behavior again. To do it in private is disrespectful and unacceptable, but to do it in front of others will not be tolerated and you will be punished for it." He gave her a hard look, hoping she understood that he had reached his boundary. "Have I made myself clear?"

"Yes," she said through gritted teeth "Good. Do not test me further."

Chapter 12

Aviva

Aviva didn't want to admit it but the feel of the soft, cool fabric against her skin was magnificent. She had never felt anything like it. The swish of the material that moved against her legs as they rode was luxurious, and Aviva had never seen a cleverer set of sashes that tied up each side of her heavy skirts to make it more comfortable to ride but kept her modesty intact. After the dress had been adjusted while she stood in the middle of the prince's suites at the Dancing Boar, she had been ushered to his room to change into the next dress and then final dress. All more wonderful than the next.

Each dress was simple in its design of a full length skirt with two light weight petticoats, a thick waist band and a tight bodice that laced up at the front. The lacing allowed her the chance to decide how much she cinched in her waist and accentuated her breasts—which was none at all. She didn't want anyone looking at her or getting an impression that she welcomed looking. The bodice had a square cut top and mid length sleeves with a minor puff on the shoulders and upper arm. Buttons sat at the top of the bodice so the over apron could be changed simply at any time. Each of the three dresses were in patterned fabrics. The one she had chosen to wear first was a two-toned checked blue, with a plain navy over apron that matched the ribbons that held her skirt up to ride and tied at the end of her sleeves. The friendly seamstress had left enough fabric for Aviva to also fashion a matching headscarf that covered most of her brown thick long curls and kept them under control.

Shai had told her he thought she looked beautiful, and when he won the gold and gems she could have as many dresses as she liked in as many colors as she liked. This had made Aviva beam at him. She had never cared for dresses and finery, but then again, she had never worn anything so soft against her skin.

They had been traveling all afternoon and Aviva was beginning to cramp in her legs from sitting in the saddle for so long. Her body was getting used to it, but definitely needed to get down and walk around for a bit. The sun was dipping toward the horizon and the shadows had grown long by the time Albertinne called a halt to their day. The plan was to camp beside the river one final night before adjusting their course and spending two days on the road and then the next in a village.

So far, Aviva's new role had been very little aside from packing up the prince's clothes at the Dancing Boar that morning and stacking the dishes up for the serving maid to come and collect them. She was silently wishing she had paid a little more attention to what Griggory had been doing at night while she was usually taking care of the horses with Laurynnse, the head groomsman.

As they stopped and the camp sprang into action, Aviva sat her horse, Pepper, and waited to be told what to do. Prince Tommofey seemed to love any opportunity to order her around, so she doubted this would be any different. It had felt good to say no to him this morning, but Aviva was also well aware she'd pushed about as far as she could. She really didn't know why she did it to him. Oh, she knew she was stubborn, but he seemed to bring out the absolute worst in her.

She patted the side of Pepper's neck and crooned softly in the mare's ear, telling her how clever she was and that she could have water very soon.

"You know the horse doesn't understand you, right?" Tommofey's condescending voice interrupted her sweet moment with the dappled mare.

"She understands me enough. So does Toby," Aviva answered, nodding her head toward the horse Tommofey sat upon. Toby's ears pricked up at his name.

Rather than sit here and be lectured, Aviva decided she would rather find out what she should be doing before she was able to retire to her and her brothers tent for the night. "What do you require of me, Your Highness?"

"Go and supervise the unloading of my belongings. Once the pavilion is erected and furniture done you can set up for my bath."

The word bath reverberated around her brain and she tried not to panic. What did he mean by set up for his bath? Gently Aviva nudged Pepper into a walk and led her over to the large cart that was drawn by two donkeys that carried all the princes must-have belongings. One of the soldiers that had been assigned to unpack the prince's things came to stand by her. "Is everything fine, My Lady?"

Aviva started at the title. No one had ever called her that aside from her father. "Oh, I'm not a lady. Just call me Viv."

"I can't do that, My Lady."

"Why ever not?"

"Prince Tommofey has told us that with your raise in station you must also be addressed in a more formal manner."

"My raise in station? My Brand is still that of a Servant." This was confusing.

"Yes, the Brand cannot be changed, but to be the personal Servant to a prince of the realm is of the highest honor, and titles come with it."

She blinked at him, trying to understand. "You really going to start calling me Lady, regardless of what I want?"

The young soldier gave her a cheeky grin. "Yes, Lady Aviva."

"I never heard anyone calling Griggory a Lord."

This brought a chuckle. "He is but twelve."

"Well, yes, but still."

"Griggory will be addressed as Squire when he is older, and then onto Steward. If we were at the palace you would be known as a Lady-in-Waiting. Hence the title, Lady."

Shai rode up and joined her.

"Do you know about this nonsense of me being called a Lady now?" she asked with a slight snort.

"Oh yes, he tried to call me a Lord, but I declined. Said I like my Warrior brand."

"And he listened to you?"

Shai shrugged. "Probably not. When does he ever listen to anyone unless it suits him?"

"True." Viv turned back to the soldier unloading the cart. "Am I supposed to be doing anything? Prince Tommofey said I should be here supervising the unloading of his belongings, but I figure you all know what you are doing without my interference."

"Dismount and give your brother the reins to your horse." Quickly Aviva did what she was told. "The pavilion is almost up." He pointed to his right and Aviva saw that they were driving home the final tent pegs. There were several men standing by holding large rolled up rugs. As she turned back, she saw the round tub being rolled to the edge of the cart. It must be the bath he mentioned before. "It won't take long to set up now. It's always the pavilion that takes the most amount of time. There is just his clothing chest and yours to go."

"My clothing chest?" she asked, bewildered.

"Those new dresses you got today, where did you think they ended up?" She blushed as she realized she hadn't really thought about it. "Those two are yours." He pointed at two ornate chests as he explained. "One for clothing and personal items, the other for your bedding, so it doesn't get wet."

"My bedding is with my brother's bedding. Stored with our tent."

"No, My Lady, your bedding is here. Your room will be set up much the same way as Griggory's was, but they might give you a little more space as your requirements are more as a grown woman."

"Sounds like you have everything in hand. Don't worry, Viv, I'll make sure Pepper is given a good comb." Shai went to tug the reins to get his horse to turn but Aviva grabbed his leg.

"No, this can't be right."

"What can't be right?" Her brother looked down at her.

"That I am now expected to sleep with the prince."

Shai laughed. "No one said you had to sleep with the prince. They said you were taking over Griggory's bed-chamber in the prince's tent. Which makes sense as he is there to serve the prince all day and night."

"And you think that is acceptable for a grown woman to be alone with a man like that?" she demanded.

Shai stopped laughing. "You can't be serious. We all know how you feel about each other. I am still amazed he even agreed to have you be his personal Servant."

Aviva just stared at him in disbelief.

"No, seriously, no one has ever said a word about im-proper behavior. He is pompous and a pain in your arse, but he is honorable."

"He better be," she said through gritted teeth.

Chapter 13

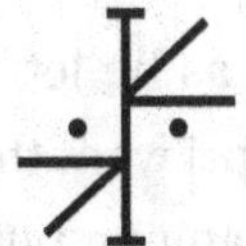

Tommofey

The space inside the pavilion was a little cramped and at first Tommofey couldn't figure out why. He frowned as he looked around. "Why is it different?" he asked Albertinne.

"Ladies need more space than men. Their clothing is larger and there are more layers. Lady Aviva has several dresses, and over aprons, plus a robe, and undergarments, as well as kerchiefs, boots, slippers, and ribbons. There is possibly a bonnet in there too."

Tommofey thought of the becoming lavender bonnet she had worn at the tournament.

"We didn't think you would want her belongings in with yours so created a little dressing room for her. It sits in between your main room and her bedchamber.

"Let me see this dressing area." Tommofey walked toward a sheet of fabric that had been hung to create a curtain. He pulled it back to reveal a narrow space with a makeshift table of two clothing chests on their sides as legs and three planks of wood to create a bench. A three-legged stool sat under the dressing table. A lantern sat on the table as well as a brush, comb, and hand mirror. Someone clever had thought of a way to string up a rope in between two poles and her clothing had been hung along the rope.

"Impressive," he said as he let the curtain drop. "Tomorrow when you set up, I want the area widened slightly and another rope for hanging put on the opposite side. My wardrobe requires airing as much as hers."

"Certainly, Your Highness."

"Good. Now, what is for supper?" he asked.

"Warmed egg and bacon pie, Your Highness," a voice said too brightly as the tent flap opened. Aviva curtsied with a flourish and smiled at the captain. I am told that I must ask if you prefer to bathe or eat first. Which one would suit you, My Lord?"

Tommofey tried to keep his surprise from showing. He had been expecting a far different attitude from Aviva. "I'll eat now, while the bath water is heating."

"Yes, Your Highness. And where do I put this?" she asked, holding up his cartography case.

"Be careful with that!" he yelped, rushing to take it from her.

Aviva blinked at him as he took the case. "I wasn't going to throw it," she defended herself.

"I didn't say you were. Stop being so god damn sensitive."

She curtsied more deeply this time. "Of course, My Lord." Her voice dripped with sarcasm. "I shall take my feminine hysterics away and see to your meal. Will you be eating inside or outside?"

Tommofey gritted his teeth. "Outside will be fine."

Without a backward glance or a pardon, Aviva spun and left the pavilion.

"And you thought this was a brilliant idea," Tom accused Albertinne.

"Brilliant may be pushing it, but it certainly fixed the situation."

"Mmmm..." The prince didn't comment further.

"I'll leave you to it then." Albertinne nodded his head and left the pavilion.

Tommofey dismissed the annoying woman from his thoughts and went to his small table to place the leather case carefully upon it. He looked forward to settling down after his bath and adding in the new area they traveled today—it had been less winding than the old map they were following had indicated, and they had managed to travel further than what they thought they would.

The next half turning went by quickly as Tommofey ate his two egg and bacon pies outside, watching the sun set from his seat underneath the small awning in front of his pavilion. The pies had come from the talented chef at the Dancing Boar and he had also managed to unearth a flagon of red that had been hidden away in the cellar by his father.

The prince had watched Aviva hurry around, organizing the water and tub, and waited until she announced his bath was ready. He entered the main area to find the set up different from Griggory's way, but effective in that everything she would require was laid within reach of the tub. The bar of fragranced soap, cleaning oils for his hair, and a large rough toweling cloth were sitting on the stool that he typically used when sitting at his table doing his cartography work. On top of the towel was several sized sponges and a pumice stone, as well as a long-handled pot for rinsing. Inviting steam rose from the tub and she had perhaps gone a little over board in adding soap flakes as there was a small amount of thick bubbles attempting to escape down the side.

"I unpacked your robe and hung it next to mine in the dressing room. I hope that was appropriate?" she asked. Rather than her usual candor, Aviva appeared nervous.

The little dressing room was going to be perfect for them to share a space for the next several weeks.

"Yes, that is acceptable," he said as he hurried to the sectioned-off area. Tom quickly undressed and dropped his clothes on the stool and makeshift table before grabbing the robe Aviva had hung for him. He walked over to the curtain and pulled it back to find Aviva heading toward the door. "Where do you think you are going?" Tommofey asked as he tied the robe belt tighter.

"Just giving you your privacy while you bathe." She stopped but didn't turn around.

"I don't need privacy, I need a personal Servant. My clothes need to be sorted and hung." He nodded his head toward the dressing area. "And you are required to wash my hair."

Aviva

She must not have heard him correctly. "You want me to do what?" Aviva tried to remain calm. This was exactly what she was afraid of. Her heart began to race.

"I want you to wash my hair," he repeated.

"You say that so calmly."

"Why would I not say it calmly?"

"You invite me into your bath to wash you and now you are trying to pretend you are the one offended."

"I wish you would stop jumping to conclusions." He sounded exasperated. "One. When did I say you should join me? Two. Why would you think I wanted you to join me? Three. I told you to wash my hair. Griggory does not get into the bath to wash my hair. Four. He manages perfectly well standing behind me and is shorter than you."

This was followed by the sound of water splashing and Tommofey letting out a sigh. Aviva bit her lip in an effort to not say anything further and add to the awkwardness of the situation. She would wash the prince's hair as ordered and maybe she could drown him in the process. Viv took a deep breath and turned around to find the tall prince sitting in the water. He didn't quite fit the tub, and he looked a little uncomfortable with his knees sticking out of the water. The water came up to his mid chest. Tommofey sat with his back leaning against the wooden tub, his arms out of the water and resting along the top of the sides. She hoped the bubbles hid everything else.

Aviva hesitated a moment longer before walking to stand behind him. She looked down at his broad expanse of naked shoulders and the strange feeling in her stomach grew. It was odd and mildly disquieting. She ignored the feeling as best she could and picked up the long-handled pot. Aviva dipped it into the water and brought it up to pour it carefully over the prince's head, fighting every instinct to simply dump it on his head and tell him to do it himself.

Aviva spent several moments making sure his hair was saturated before she put the pot down and picked up the cleansing oil. The smell of lavender and rosemary filled the tent and it was calming and wonderful. The feel of the oil as it lathered in her palm was remarkable, nothing she had ever held created bubbles so big.

It took her two attempts and a silent stern reprimand before Aviva found the courage to reach out and touch his hair. She had never touched a man other than her brother and father. Men had touched her, but she had never invited it and usually slapped their hand away as soon they even looked to be reaching for her. It was possibly the only reason in her opinion to get married so men stopped touching her. Though, she also was well aware that the Servant brand made her more of a target to the soldiers, who would more than likely never touch a woman with the Common brand, as the servant brand was the lowest caste and abused more frequently without consequences. Another reason to hate the Gods and their brands.

Slowly she massaged the oil into his thick, light brown hair, scrubbing her nails across his scalp to loosen the dirt. Aviva felt a stirring lower in her stomach, closer to the apex where her legs joined and the warmth that spread was wonderful but also made her feel uneasy. She watched the lather from the oil glide slowly down Tommofey's long refined neck and onto his collarbone before it slid down the front of his chest, leaving a trail of bubbles that for no reason she wanted to trace her finger along.

"You need to rinse and do it again," he said into the silence, breaking into her daydream.

Aviva started at the sound of his voice. "Yes, My Lord," she murmured softly. Slowly so as to not disturb the water too much nor the bubbles that hid her seeing anything she shouldn't, Aviva dipped the long-handled pot into the water and dribbled it over his head. The idea of *accidentally* dumping the entire pot on his head and making him splutter was appealing, but she decided to behave. After the scene she had created in the suite this morning, in front of the seamstress, Viv was still very aware of his threat of punishment if she didn't tow the line.

As she began to lather in a second lot of oil, Aviva began to hum to herself—a soft, gentle tune that she only used when she was content, usually when she was hiding in the stables, surrounded by the horses. It took her a few moments to realize that Tommofey was humming with her, and instead of stopping, she took extra time in massaging his scalp and enjoying the odd feeling that seemed to be spreading inside her.

After she rinsed the second lot of oil from him, Aviva picked up a wide-tooth comb and pulled it through his hair, feeling the silky strands run over her fingers she almost sighed with contentment. "Hand me the soap," Tommofey instructed, holding out his hand. Viv did as she was told. She averted her eyes as she watched him slide the yellow bar over his shoulders, her insides tightening in a way that made her eyes open wider in wonder.

"Here," he said, and she looked up to find the prince holding out the soap. "Take it and don't wrap it until to-morrow morning. We want it to dry out. It is less wasteful that way."

As she hurried to do as he bid, deciding that putting it in the dressing room where it could dry without it getting on anything, but also adding the bonus of having it in an enclosed space so it's lovely fragrance would hopefully permeate her clothing. She looked at his pile of clothes he had dumped onto the makeshift shelf and stool. She would come back and hang the garments as soon as his bath was complete.

A figure loomed behind her, causing a dark shadow to fill the narrow space. Aviva let out a little squeak and turned quickly. It was Tommofey, standing in nothing more than a towel wrapped around his hips. His chest glistened in the lamplight and she quickly looked down at her feet.

"If we are to share a living space you will be required to bathe every evening. You currently smell like horse and dirt." His voice was matter-of-fact.

Aviva, as always, responded by feeling personally attacked. "My, my, you are full of compliments." She brought her eyes up to meet his hazel ones. "You should have said something before. I will catch a chill if I bathe in the river now, after all the sun has set." Aviva fought hard to keep the derision from her voice. He really was an imbecile if he thought she was going to wash in a river after the sun had set. She would also have to find a time when it was convenient for her brother to watch out for her, like they had been doing the past week of travel when required.

Tommofey stepped away from the dressing room. "You can stay in here and clean while I get dressed out there. Tomorrow my clothes will be placed in here too. It will be more convenient for everyone."

He let the fabric settle back into place and Aviva busied herself picking up and folding his clothing. She hung his heavy cloak over the end of the wooden pole and placed the folded shirt and trousers on the table, being careful to keep it away from the wet soap. His undergarments she put in a separate pile and decided that she would launder his when she laundered her own.

"I am going to inspect the troops," he spoke from the other side of the curtain.

Aviva lifted the fabric out of the way to see him. "Do you require your cloak?"

"Yes." He took the dark heavy cloak from the hook she had put it on. "You have a half turning to wash yourself." He adjusted the cloak and then stopped and raised an eyebrow at her. "Unless you would like me to stay and wash your hair for you?" he offered, clear merriment in his voice.

Aviva almost fell for it but caught herself just in time. He was teasing her, after her assumptions earlier. "No, thank you for the offer though." She waved airily, two could play at this game. "If I require your services I will let you know."

"Yes, My Lady." His tone was mocking. His face turned serious. "Remember, half a turning and I want this cleaned up. I have things that require my attention after that. Use the soap and hair oils too." He wrinkled his nose at her before walking out the pavilion.

Viv huffed at him and his rudeness as she followed him out and came to stand by the tub. As she bent and trailed her hand through the still pleasantly warm water she smiled and began to hum to herself again. She supposed she could get used to this part of the role.

Chapter 14

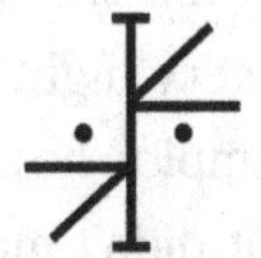

Tommofey

Prince Tommofey attempted to ignore the contented humming coming from the inside of his tent. He did everything in his power not to think about the naked woman that was soaping herself in his tub. He ran his hand over his damp hair and shifted in his seat to hide his erection under the cloth napkin that draped across his lap. The past two days had been blissful torture and completely unexpected. Tommofey's feelings towards the demanding, clever, quick-witted and too-opinionated sister of his Champion were complicated and something he was actively avoiding in the hope he was just lonely.

He pushed his meal aside and picked up the goblet, taking a sip he tried to bring his focus back to what was in front of him. Shai and Pynnan were practicing hand-to-hand combat, and he couldn't tell who was winning. They would grapple for a while and then someone would inevitably tap the person or the ground and they would break apart, stand, and start again. It was interesting to watch, but he didn't see the point of it.

Finally, Pynnan called for a break and both men stood, talking quietly while another soldier of lower rank offered them ale or water. Tommofey watched as Pynnan took the water while Shai took the jug of ale. It had been reported to him that every night since the Warrior had been chosen as the Champion he had drunk with the men before going to sleep. It didn't matter who was on duty there was always someone off duty to agree to a drink with him. Tom didn't know if he should be concerned or not. Perhaps he should speak to Captain Albertinne about it, but then he hated to admit he didn't know everything.

Shai noticed the prince watching and grasped Pynnan on the shoulder before heading in Tommofey's direction.

"Your Highness," he said in way of greeting.

"Shai." He inclined his head at his Champion. Tommofey was always a little uncomfortable in the man's presence, though he knew Shai should feel honored to fight for him, it was now only truly sinking in what would happen if he faltered.

"Is that my sister humming?" Shai sounded mildly surprised as he peered at the closed tent flaps.

"Yes, I allow her to bathe once I am done with mine. As you can tell she seems to quite enjoy herself."

"I haven't heard that song for many years. It was a favorite of our mother's."

"It appears Lady Aviva likes it too." Prince Tommofey took another sip of his wine. "Tell me, why do you fight Pynnan like that? Where are your swords?"

"We must hone all of our techniques. What happens if I drop my sword or we get there and there has been a rule change and I am not allowed to use it? Hand-to-hand combat is an essential thing to know. Your father taught me much in the ways of the Pomaikkan's which was taught to him by a trusted soldier. But I worry that my opponent will have had more training, or better training." Shai drained his cup. "I know I seem cocky and have belief in my abilities, but one must also have humility enough to continue to learn when the opportunity is presented. Lieutenant Pynnan was bested by me, but I can still learn from him."

"That is sound thinking." An idea began to form in Tommofey's mind. "I would like to learn to defend myself. As of tomorrow, each time when we arrive in camp and while everyone is occupied with setting up, I want you to teach me some basic sword work."

Shai bowed. "It would be an honor to teach the son of my first teacher. However, tomorrow we will be in the village of Ripperedst."

Tommofey waved his hand. "The next day then."

Shai bowed. "Yes, My Lord."

Aviva

The tent was filled with the content humming of the prince, making Aviva smile as she folded the final item over the makeshift line and stood back satisfied with how the dressing room looked. In the few short days they had been sharing living space they had managed to come to an understanding of who needed to be where to keep some semblance of privacy while she remained available to his princely whims. Though, surprisingly, the whims were less than she had anticipated.

Sitting down at the dressing table, Aviva picked up her brush and ran it through her hair, before swapping to the comb and then finally her fingers, where she spent some time scrunching her long hair to bring her curls out. She found herself singing softly to the tune Prince Tommofey hummed and she closed her eyes for a second and pretended that she wasn't his Servant but instead his lover who he was now preparing to woo with candles and flowers. Blushing, she opened her eyes and frowned at herself in her small hand mirror. Where had that idea come from? That was not appropriate in any way. Seeing his naked torso each day was clearly having an impact on her thoughts and making her consider things that were ridiculous to consider. He was a prince, and she was a Servant, and he had made it clear that she was nothing more than that to him. She was here to serve because her brother had blackmailed him and Griggory had got sick. It was that simple, there was no romantic undertones that he was hiding.

Her flush made her forehead glisten and she pressed the back of her hand to it. She had been warm all afternoon, but even to her she felt hot. Aviva fanned herself with the mirror and picked up the towel she had placed next to her to wipe her forehead. Aviva looked at the dress she had been planning on wearing for the evening but changed her mind. She was far too hot to wear it. Instead, she would put on her nightgown and her robe. If she went straight from the dressing room to her small sectioned off bed chamber the prince probably wouldn't even notice her.

She was tired too. Viv had been hoping that the bath would revive her, but it had been the opposite, it was like it had drained last of her energy. Perhaps if Tommofey was so involved in his note taking that he did every night he would be happy for her to simply go to bed. Usually there was little she did for him after he had bathed and eaten, it was the only time she became lonely. Aviva even missed the company of the two gossips she had shared a room with back in the garrison. But tonight she didn't care, she just wanted to lie down for a moment.

The satin of the new night dress she had been given was cooling against her skin, and Aviva relished it as she pulled on the matching navy robe. It was a shimmery material with a silver thread through it, and Aviva was still astounded that it had been provided for her. If the prince had not been so clear in his disinterest of her she may have been worried, but he had dismissed her concerns and proven his words so many times she had finally stopped worrying about him wanting more from her. The oddest thing had happened though, as soon as Aviva had realized he really didn't want to do anything with her she wanted to know why. It made absolutely no sense to her, but there it was. Why didn't he find her attractive?

Aviva tidied up her belongings and tried to sneeze quietly. Her nose began to run, and she looked around to find something to blow it on. One of the prince's monogrammed kerchiefs was poking out his waistcoat pocket, that was hung ready to be worn tomorrow. Needing something to stem the flow, she took the white linen cloth and pressed it to her nose.

Slowly Aviva opened the curtain, so as to not disturb the prince. She stopped a moment to watch him and the transformation of his face as he drew in his book. It was the only time he looked his eighteen years, and carefree. His light brown hair flopped down over his face and his tongue stuck out to the side of his mouth as he concentrated on whatever he was drawing. Her curiosity had been killing her for days about what he did, but for some reason she was hesitant to ask.

Holding the kerchief to her nose, Aviva walked to her left to the next curtain that was the entrance to her own bedchamber. She slid into the darkened space, not bothering to light the lantern that sat on the low crate next to her bed. She was beginning to tremble and was feeling cool now, so kept her robe on and crawled into the many blankets that made her bed the most comfortable thing she had ever slept on, and without a further thought Aviva went to sleep.

She woke several times throughout the night alternating between hot and sweaty, and shivering and chilled. It was clear that she had picked up whatever Griggory had had, but was too tired to think about it. She just kept telling herself as she woke up coughing that she was tougher than him, and would be fine if she just got enough rest.

"I warned you you would get sick," Tom grumbled as he looked at Aviva struggling to pack his clothes. She had fumbled twice to tuck his boots into the pack, clumsily dropping one on the floor as she sneezed. "You kept me awake with your coughing." He watched as she bent to pick up the boot. "Leave it and come here," he ordered.

Aviva did what she was told. She stopped about two feet away from him, aware of how small the space in the dressing room was when he was in there with her. She rarely stood this close to him and facing him. Typically he was sitting, eating, working, riding, or in the bath. If he was standing it was further away from her. He was so tall, but Aviva was too tired to look at him, so she just stared at the button on his shirt.

Without warning, Tommofey's hand took her gently by the chin and tilted her head back, he pressed his hand against her forehead. "You're burning up."

She could feel a coughing attack coming on and didn't want to cough on him so took a step back and pushed him away, turning her head and coughing into her sleeve. Aviva tried to take a breath, but it hurt to breathe too deeply, and it made her cough harder.

The prince left. *Probably to not get sick,* Aviva thought as she wiped her nose with the kerchief she had taken the previous night. Tommofey barged back into the dressing room holding a goblet. "Here, it's water." He held it out to her, but it took her a few moments to stop coughing enough to take it from him.

"Thank you," she wheezed through small sips of the cooling water. "Just give me a moment and I will be fine—" Aviva began to cough again. "I'm a little dizzy, I just need to—" The room was getting darker and her head lighter. The prince's face came very close to her own and she blinked up at him, noticing how beautiful his hazel eyes were. "I just need to..." Aviva tried to get the words out, but the next thing she knew she was falling and everything was going dark.

Chapter 15

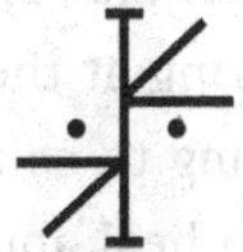

Tommofey

"Can we really afford to wait, Your Highness?" Captain Albertinne asked as he and Tommofey stepped out of the pavilion. They had left Shai to undress his sister and make her more comfortable. The prince had caught Aviva as she passed out and laid her on his bed rather than try to negotiate the small space in her bed chamber. He had then called out to the guards at the tent opening for someone to get Shai and Albertinne. Tommofey had insisted to Shai that Aviva was to stay in the prince's bed as it would be easier for those who would take care of her to get to her.

Tommofey was torn and completely unprepared for his emotions when it came to the sick woman. He had not hesitated to leave Griggory behind, but Aviva was a different matter. "We don't have a great deal of choice. Shai won't leave his sister while she is ill, and I am not sure if you have noticed, but he sort of has me at a disadvantage." Tom kept his voice low.

"But the chirurgeon told you that Griggory would need four days to recover, we don't have four days," Albertinne reminded him unnecessarily.

While he had waited for Shai and Albertinne to arrive, Tommofey had sat staring at the beautiful passed out woman on his bed, trying to come up with a plan that would give her time to heal and still get them to the Arena on time. He had pulled out the map of the area he had been using and his case to do a few calculations of possible scenarios. This had done a great deal in keeping his anxiety at bay.

Tommofey looked at the heavy-set Captain. "Look at the big picture. We have just over three and a half weeks to get to the Arena. We have made up a little time already. If we take two or three days to rest and wait for her to recover, we can make up those days by starting a little earlier in the morning and riding till dusk at night. I have been studying the terrain of the area, and believe with some minor adjustments it can be done. We just can't afford for more mishaps."

"Perhaps we can send two men ahead and have the items prepared so we don't have to stay in the villages if we need to push through, have the supplies ready for us to pick up and keep moving," added Albertinne.

Tommofey didn't like the idea of forgoing the comfort of real food but held his tongue. "There are only two more villages before we head into the forest and onto the Arena, so we must prepare carefully as to not miss anything."

"By the look of Lady Aviva we are going to have at least two days to prepare."

"I hate to admit it, but I think you are correct."

"Do you want me to have another tent set up for her? Mine is larger than most. She could have mine, and I will bunk in with Shai and we can assign one of the grooms-men to see to your needs." Albertinne reasoned.

"No, leave her where she is. I have already been exposed to whatever she has, and think it unlikely if I didn't pick it up from Griggory that I will pick it up from her. I can get by without a Servant for a few days if we stay here. Everything is already set up after all. We should keep her isolated."

Shai cleared his throat as he came out of the tent. "She is awake and speaking nonsense." He shook his head and smiled to himself. "Keeps claiming that you should leave her here to fend for herself. That she will be fine."

Tommofey shook his head. "Does she truly think me a monster?"

"My sister does love a little drama, and when she is unwell even more so. Though, to be honest, I think her fever is making her slightly delusional."

This brought a laugh from all three men. "If that will be all and you have decided, My Lord, I will have the men broken up into groups. We will need to hunt for more food, gather more firewood and might as well take the time to check over our equipment and horses."

"Yes, that will be all." Tom stopped for a moment and then added. "Oh, and have cook make a broth for Lady Aviva."

Albertinne saluted and walked away. Tommofey looked to Shai. "I know you have been with your sister now, but I would prefer, if at all possible, to keep you not too close. We can't afford to have anyone else get sick and hold us up even longer. You can of course visit her, but perhaps not sit close to her?"

"Then who will take care of her?" Shai's concern was evident and heart-warming. Tommofey wished there was someone that cared about him as much as these siblings clearly cared for each other. There was his mother, but on more than one occasion Tom had wondered if she cared about him or what he represented. Did she see him for him? Shai and Aviva loved each other and saw their flaws as not something to be shunned but accepted and loved as part of them. It was not something Tommofey had witnessed so openly before.

"If you are okay with it, I will care for her." Prince Tommofey said the words slowly; he couldn't quite believe they were coming from his mouth. "The chirurgeon was clear on how to care for Griggory and we will do the same for Lady Aviva."

"Are you sure?" Shai said doubtfully. "You are a Prince, and she is but a Servant."

"She is your sister and she needs to be well. I am the logical choice."

A smirk crossed Shai's face "Very well, I wish you luck."

"Luck? Why luck?" Tommofey asked, all of a sudden feeling slightly less sure of his choice.

"Have you met my sister?" Shai laughed and shook his head.

Prince Tommofey wondered what exactly he had just volunteered for.

Aviva scowled at him. "I don't want any broth."

"Well, that's too bad because that is what you are having," Tommofey kept his tone neutral.

"Says who?"

"Says me."

Aviva pouted and sniffed before dabbing at her nose with her kerchief. Tommofey noted the PT embroidered in the corner and raised an eyebrow at her. "Where did you get the kerchief?" he asked.

Her watery eyes looked at the offending kerchief and then back at him. "It was either your kerchief or the sleeve on your jacket. I was desperate," she admitted.

He wanted to be angry, but looking at how miserable she looked he couldn't do it. "Fine, if you eat half a bowl of broth, you can keep the kerchief. Eat the whole thing and I will give you another one," he bribed her.

Aviva even in her weakened state glowered at him for several moments.

"Fine," she agreed. "Give me the bowl."

She pulled herself up and settled herself against his cushions and held out her hands. But all the movement had brought on another coughing fit.

Tommofey held the bowl away from her. "I will hold it. All you need is one coughing fit and you will be wearing it." He carefully took the spoon and half-filled it, wiping the base on the edge before holding it out for her to eat off. Aviva stared at him for a few moments before she opened her mouth and allowed him to feed her.

"There, that didn't kill you," he observed.

"Must be killing you, though," she countered.

Tommofey chose not to answer. Instead, he offered her another spoonful of the clear broth. Aviva eyed it warily before giving in and taking the mouthful.

"Why are you doing this?" she asked after swallowing the second spoonful.

Tommofey shrugged, pretending he had no clue what she meant. He didn't want to think about the complicated emotions this woman brought up in him.

"You know that's not an answer, right?" Aviva stared at him expectantly.

"I am doing it because I don't want your brother to get sick, or anyone else. I need to be at the Arena on time, and we can't have any more hold ups. I figured I didn't get sick when Griggory did and have been sharing space with you for several days, so I should have got it if I was going to by now." Tommofey offered her another spoonful of soup.

Aviva took it and settled back on the cushions even further. "Whose idea was it?"

"Why does that matter?" he asked.

"I don't know. Probably doesn't." Aviva turned her head away from him and coughed.

"It was my idea," he said softly.

"Because you need to get to the Arena on time," she reaffirmed.

"Yes, or what is the point of the whole thing?" he pointed out.

"To prove that you are worthy of your mother's love and sacrifices?" Her voice was barely audible, he almost didn't hear it.

The words stung, but he didn't refute them. Instead, Tommofey offered Aviva another spoonful of broth. Silence grew around them as he continued to feed her, and the only sound was her occasional cough.

"That was rude of me." Aviva finally broke the awkward silence. "I am sure the Lady Darria loves you and is proud of you. After all, from the small amount I have been told it seems she was a good queen. Compassionate and kind."

"I have been told that too, but it saddens me to say that she is no longer like that. A high ranking priest told me that my mother was once warm and considerate, and loved by many."

"See." Aviva smiled kindly.

Tom shook his head. "No, because in the next breath the same priest told me my mother had drugged and imprisoned the Seer for her own personal use. And the worst thing was when I asked her about it she didn't deny it, just made up excuses as to why that was acceptable."

"You really going to get all high and mighty about your mother when you go around threatening people and using the excuse that you are the rightful heir and a prince to get away with it?"

"Do you really think I am going to drug and imprison someone for my own ends?" he asked seriously.

Aviva studied him for a moment, her lovely brown eyes taking in his whole face. He didn't flinch under the scrutiny. He knew he was a pompous ass who threw around his title, but the thought of drugging someone to get his own way was disgusting, and it was only now discussing it with Aviva did he see his mother through the priest's eyes. And it wasn't pleasant.

"When your brother came and said that he wouldn't leave without you what did I do?" he asked her.

"You barged into my room and ordered me around." She lifted her chin and glared at him.

This made Tommofey laugh. "Even deathly ill you will be difficult." Aviva narrowed her eyes. "Did I order you held captive and force your brother to fight for me and only if he won would you be set free?"

"Shai would not have fought for you."

Prince Tommofey put the soup bowl down on the crate that served as a bedside table and leaned in, so they were close. "That's the thing. He would have fought for you to remain safe. If I was a different man, I would have banished you to Pluddgish and blackmailed your brother to fight for me or he never sees you again and I throw you into a whore house." He sat back and picked up the bowl of soup. "But what happened? I let him blackmail me into bringing you along and I don't think you have been treated in any other way but fairly."

Aviva took the proffered broth without complaint. Tommofey was so intent on not spilling any broth he didn't realize she had reached out to touch him until he felt her hand on his thigh. He looked down at her hand and then up at her. She smiled sadly at him.

"What your mother went through must have been horrendous. Absolutely heartbreaking. Month after month of not conceiving. Year after year of failing at the one thing she was required to do. The whole country waiting for her and then to finally be cast aside by the king so he can remarry and hopefully make an heir only for him to choose her sister. Soul destroying." Aviva's voice was barely above a whisper. "That has to change someone."

Tommofey nodded. "Yes, especially as she loved my father and he, from all I have been told, loved her. I still don't understand it, and no one will talk about it."

She squeezed his leg. "I am sorry."

"Thank you. It is confusing. I love her and she has done so much for me, but she also pushes me to be King and..." He let the words trail off, afraid of what would happen if he spoke his thoughts aloud. "It does not matter now. Shai will fight and win, I will be crowned, my mother will be happy, and you will have me out of your hair and able to go live your life how you wish." He held up the final spoonful of broth which she took without complaint. "And you have now earned two kerchiefs from me."

Chapter 16

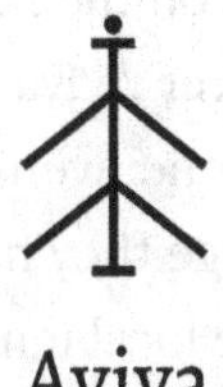

Aviva

It still amazed Aviva how quickly her life had changed in the past month. She had gone from being a Servant in the garrison in Binttle to the personal Servant to Prince Tommofey, one of the claimants to the throne of Segarris. Not only did she now carry the title of Lady, but she also had new clothing that went with the title and had been nursed back to health by the prince himself. She could only imagine how green with envy both Nikkitta and Lyubbov would have been had they known about it.

They had been back on the road for five days after waiting for her to recover for three. No one said anything to her, but she could feel the pressure building in all of them as the appointed date grew closer and they all prayed for nothing further to go wrong. Even after Tommofey's initial "I told you so" about going near the sick Griggory he had refrained from any other antagonistic comments.

While Viv had been sick, her brother had visited every night, sitting at the small table the prince used for his journal writing or whatever he did that he kept so secret. She had on several occasions tried to broach the subject but didn't know where to begin, it was killing her to not know what he was recording or painting in that little book of his.

Once they were back on the road, Shai had continued to arrive each night after Aviva had bathed and eaten. The siblings had spent the evenings laughing and reminiscing. At the last village they had passed through they had purchased from the local inn keeper his board set of pawns and kings as well as his last flagon of red wine. Now the three of them, and once or twice Captain Albertinne had joined them, to play each other as the weather had changed and it had begun to rain most nights.

Aviva was only half paying attention to the game the prince and her brother were playing as she sat on the edge of the prince's bed, sipping the wine Prince Tommofey had insisted they all try, and enjoying the slight light headedness and glow she was getting from it.

"Tell me about my father," Tommofey said, his words casual.

Shai's hand stilled for a moment over the tower piece he was about to move. "What would you like to know?"

Aviva watched Tommofey. She was getting better at reading him. He was nowhere near as callous and pompous as she had first assumed. Inside was a young man lost about who he was and hoping to please the only person who had ever shown him love, however toxic it was. Her heart had softened toward him in every way, but she had no intention of letting him know that. She was also secretly willing to admit that he was the first man she found attractive and had even started to find herself thinking up ways that she could stay in his company as they traveled throughout the day. The few moments she got to spend each night with him, washing his hair and admiring his naked shoulders, had begun to appear in her dreams at night. Dreams that would have made her blush and dismiss just mere weeks ago, but now she wished they would be true.

"Did he talk about me?" Tommofey's voice was quiet, and Aviva's heart reached out to him—the sad little boy who didn't know where he belonged, who people gossiped about while his mother proclaimed to all who would listen that he was the rightful heir.

"Yes, he spoke of you. On one occasion I was privileged to share a meal and ale with him after a sparring session. Your father had a little too much to drink and he spoke about why he spent so much time away from the capital, overseeing and fighting the small skirmishes that would take place between the marauders and locals on the Islands of Lobbregath. I have never seen a man more conflicted." Shai looked at the Prince with the same compassion that Aviva was feeling. Her brother continued to speak. "The king was torn between his duty, his love for all his sons, and the love for a woman he had hurt more deeply and his feelings of guilt whenever he saw her. The whole thing was a complicated mess that he knew he had created, and in the end was a coward who would rather stay away than deal with the fall out of his actions. He was a deeply flawed man, but he loved your mother and you very much."

"He loved us?"

Aviva's eyes began to tear up as she watched Tommofey grapple with what Shai had just said.

"Yes, and your brothers. He regretted not seeing you grow but was always aware of your achievements. He talked about your love of maps and how it began with you sending him a note asking him to send a drawing of where he was. He sent you a compass and a map."

"He did and I still carry it with me."

Understanding dawned for Aviva. The leather case held a compass. Tommofey's obsession with the small case he carried and making certain all its contents were stacked properly was important because it was his only connection with his father.

"Would you like to see it?" he asked shyly.

"Very much," Shai said. The exchange was sweet, and Aviva found herself smiling as Tommofey went to get the case he had stored in the crate next to his bed.

As Aviva watched the prince eagerly explain to both her and Shai what each item in the case did and proudly showed them the compass that had come from the king, she finally understood that in many ways Tommofey was just as stuck as she was. He was not free to do what he wished. He was trapped by convention and his mother to do what was required. She was trapped by her brand. His cage was just prettier than hers, but in the end, it was still a cage.

"**W**hy don't you have double letters in your name?" Tommofey asked while he continued to study the game board.

"Huh?" she said, only half paying attention. She had been watching his hands hover over the game pieces and imagining what it would be like if they touched her in a loving way.

"I asked why you and Shai don't have double letters in your given names? It is unusual."

"It is a normal thing on the Lobbregath Islands and since we were born there, mother felt she should follow the custom. I don't think she ever intended for us to live anywhere but Pluddgish."

"I am sorry about your mother and father." His voice was gentle, like it had been when she was sick.

"I am sorry about the situation you are in and that your father never had the courage to tell you how wrong he was and that he regretted the mess he had made." Aviva tucked her hands under her thighs to stop herself from reaching up and caressing his handsome face.

"Thank you."

"Excuse me, Your Highness." The guard on duty cleared his throat as he entered the tent.

"Yes?"

"Your Champion has sent word that he won't be joining you tonight. He has decided an early night is needed."

"More likely he has found a card game and ale with one of the off-duty soldiers," Aviva muttered.

"Thank you." Prince Tommofey nodded his acknowledgement and the soldier saluted and backed out of the tent.

They both returned to the game. "Are you ready for the forest tomorrow? No more villages or towns to get your red wines and fancy cheeses," she teased.

"I am sure I will manage." He moved his horse piece and sat back to watch her. "What about you? You ever been in a big scary forest before? With all the wolves and bears out there waiting to eat you?"

Aviva looked down at the board and realized she was one move away from being beaten.

"I'm more worried about all the gloating you are going to do when you win again," she retorted. Aviva moved her king, knowing that it would only prolong the inevitable.

Tommofey smirked at her before sitting forward and lazily moving his queen.

"I don't gloat."

"Ha!" Aviva moved her king back a square, knowing the outcome but she would not just give up.

"You must be thinking of another prince." He casually moved his tower and sat back with his arms crossed.

Aviva glared at him before she gave up and tipped over her king, signally that he had won.

"I don't know any other princes. Thank the Gods, because one is enough of a handful."

Tommofey raised his eyebrow at her but didn't rise to the bait. "Another?" he asked, nodding his head toward the board.

"No, thank you, I have had enough humiliation for one evening."

"What would you like to do?" he asked.

This surprised Aviva as he had never bothered to ask what she would like; he only ever told her what he wanted. Before she lost her courage she blurted out, "I would very much like to see your map journal. You showed us last night the magnificent things your father sent, but I would love to see more of what you have created."

The response Aviva received was entirely unexpected. Tommofey beamed at her, his hazel eyes bright. It was as if this was the first time someone had genuinely cared what he did, and it broke her heart a little.

His enthusiasm was clear as he rushed to grab the small journal, and in a more animated tone than she had ever witnessed he pulled his stool around to sit next to her and handed Aviva the treasured book.

"I have been mapping each area I have passed through since the journey began. I know I showed you some of the pictures but I didn't want to bore you and Shai with all the other stuff yesterday."

"Oh, no, it's not boring at all. Please, tell me everything."

"Each day I not only draw new details of the area, but I also like to add my personal observations." He leaned over to point at the notes he had jotted down. "I like to think of ways the places I see could be planned better or what a place is lacking." He shrugged and pulled away "I guess I just like to look at things logically."

"Nothing wrong with that," Aviva said. She looked at his perfect handwriting and the magnificent pictures he had painted that made the snippets of maps he was creating look like mini masterpieces.

Tommofey stood and walked over to where he kept his personal items stored and pulled out a rolled up scroll that he spent a lot of time studying each night. He placed a weight on each corner and then took the book from her and turned it to the last page.

"As you can see, the forest we are about to enter isn't the most detailed." He pointed to the old map he had rolled out and then to the page he was currently working on in comparison. "Even though we are on a tight schedule I am hoping that I am able to still map out the area in more detail."

His hand brushed hers as they both traced the small river that they were following. Tommofey turned his face to look at her. He was so close, their faces mere inches apart as they both leaned over the map. Aviva licked her bottom lip as she watched him. And for a few moments it was as if her mind completely lost control of the situation and her emotions took over. Aviva leaned in closer and brushed her lips against his. Feeling the softness of his touch, his shallow breathing matching her own, made her core heat quickly. Aviva pulled back to look at him, startled at the way her body was feeling. Her eyes searched his for any clue to what he was thinking or feeling.

"Why did you do that?" he asked, breaking the tension.

Embarrassment flooded her and Aviva stepped back. "Your Highness," she said and bowed deeply, hoping to cover the blush that was rapidly moving up her face. "Please forgive me, it was inappropriate and..." Her voice trailed off. Aviva had no idea how she was going to re-cover from this. She had actually kissed a prince without consent. She wondered if she could be executed for such a transgression. Without another word she picked up her full skirt and ran for the privacy of her small bed chamber.

"Wait," he called, but she didn't stop. Hot tears began to fall as she swiftly closed the curtain behind her. Before Aviva could do anything other than regret her decision, the material was whisked open and Tommofey stood be-fore her. His impressive frame and height dwarfing her and making her already tiny bed chamber feel miniscule. "I told you to wait," he growled.

Aviva wiped her tears and sniffed. "I said I was sorry."

"You are impossible." Tommofey's voice was so low and rough she thought she felt the earth shake. He swept her up in his arms and pressed her body to his, crushing his mouth against hers. His tongue forced his way into her mouth and demanded her attention. Aviva didn't fight, instead she allowed herself to respond with the same passion. She reached up and twined her hand in his hair, while her other hand held fast to the front of his shirt.

Tommofey broke the kiss and pulled his head back to look at her. He did not put her down. "I thought you hated me, which is why I asked you why you kissed me."

She swallowed hard around the lump that had formed in her throat and smiled up at him. Aviva was back on familiar ground. "I wouldn't say hate exactly. My mother told me you should never hate anyone."

He slowly let her slide down until her feet were once again touching the ground. "Well, what would you say then?" His tone was light showing she hadn't broken the mood.

Screwing up all her courage and throwing all caution to the wind, Viv reached up and unbuttoned the topmost button on the prince's shirt. "Loathe would be the first word."

"Really?" he murmured but didn't stop her.

Her hands trembled slightly as she moved to the next button. "Despise."

"Go on," he urged.

She reached for the third button. "Abhor."

"Did you have to look that one up?"

The fourth and final button she fumbled before it came undone. "Detest." Aviva slowly lifted her hands and hesitated a moment before she reached out and took hold of the open lapels of the shirt and pushed them back until his gorgeous shoulders were revealed. His shirt fell onto the edge of her bed as they took up the small space of the floor.

Aviva went to touch his chest but he took both her hands and brought them up to his mouth. Tommofey kissed each palm. "You don't have to do this. You don't have to do anything you don't want to."

"I know. The moment I realized that you were never going to force me to do anything I really didn't want to do was the moment all my extreme dislike for you ended."

"Then why all the smart mouth?" He brought her hands down but didn't let go.

"Because you are still a bombastic, self-important pain in my arse."

This brought a laugh from the prince. "My goodness you sure do know how to make a man feel wanted."

Now was the time to make her confession before she lost all her courage. Her voice was barely above a whisper as she spoke. "I want you to be my first."

"How?" He sounded shocked. "How has someone as beautiful as you, who lives in a garrison full of strong, athletic men of all ages and appearances, not found someone you found appealing enough to..." He didn't finish the sentence.

Aviva shrugged. "Please don't make me answer that."

Tommofey dropped her hands and gathered her gently in his arms.

"If it makes you feel any better, I am not that experienced. My mother had me deflowered at fifteen, she said it was for my own good. Told me it would stop me skirt-chasing and getting anyone accidentally pregnant. For a year after that someone would turn up in my bed chamber once a month to keep my needs at bay. In the end it was more awkward than anything else and I would pay and dismiss them without doing anything."

A wave of revulsion for Tommofey's mother swept over her before it was replaced with a strong feeling of pity for the young man who had been told who he should be, what he should want, and even who he should bed his entire life. Aviva softly kissed his naked chest and whispered, "Tonight it is just you and me. Aviva and Tommofey. No titles or brands."

Gently he let go of her and reached up to remove the kerchief that kept her curls from falling in her face. "I adore your hair." He twined one of the curls around his finger. "And this one curl that always manages to escape and nestle against your neck." Tommofey lowered his head and kissed Aviva under her ear. He trailed soft kisses across her jawline and up onto her parted lips.

Her hands slid up his chest and onto his shoulders, the same shoulders she dreamed about caressing every night as she washed his hair. Was this really happening? Tommofey moved his hands to undo her over apron and Aviva's stomach fluttered with longing as his shoulder muscles moved and stretched under her hands. A groan escaped her, and she didn't care.

Tommofey kissed her deeply, his tongue swirling around hers. Aviva clung to his shoulders as he began to tug on the laces that held the top half of her dress up. It didn't take him long to have it loosened enough that they broke apart and he helped her take the dress off over her head. He stopped and looked at her corset and petticoat. "My goodness, how many layers do you have?"

This made her laugh. "You take care of you, and I will take care of me. Deal?"

"Done," he agreed, reaching for his boots.

With a few giggles and huffing and puffing they both managed to get their clothing off without knocking the other one over in the tiny space, their clothes tossed out the curtain and into the main area of the tent. Aviva shivered with the coolness of the night and the anticipation of what was to come. She climbed onto her bed while Tommofey shuttered the lantern so it gave off minimal light. The confined space was now filled with shadows and Aviva dragged the blanket over her. She felt Tommofey settle beside her and she reached out and tucked the blanket over him too.

"Now what?" she asked nervously.

"Now you relax and trust me."

Aviva was lying on her back and Tommofey rolled to lay on his side and face her. She felt him move towards her and lean down, his lips touched hers in the most tender kiss and everything she was worried about floated away. She was safe.

His hand settled on her hip, while he lifted his top leg and placed it over hers. Tommofey continued to kiss her with no urgency, all his earlier passion replaced with an intimacy that was intoxicating. Aviva responded to his kisses by opening her mouth and exploring him with her tongue.

Tommofey's hand moved off her hip and began to trail up her stomach towards her breasts. His hand slowly kneaded her breast, and he broke their kiss and moved so he could bend and take her nipple into his mouth while he continued to pinch and roll her other nipple between his fingers. Aviva had never felt such pleasure and she found herself pushing against him while she rolled her hips.

A groan escaped her and she closed her eyes and enjoyed each sensation. While Tommofey's mouth moved to her other nipple, his hand made its way back down her stomach to come to rest at the top of her legs. Aviva felt the leg he had rested on hers slowly pull hers to the side until she lay with her legs open, one of them trapped between his legs. Tommofey moved his hand down until he stopped again and slowly moved his fingers in a gentle circle. The feeling was intense and unexpected and Aviva bucked against his hand.

The prince let go of her nipple with his mouth and moved back up to her ear. He whispered in her ear as he began to move his fingers again, this time with a little more pressure. "That is your clit, and you never want to be with a man who doesn't know where or what it is."

By this point, all Aviva could do was nod and moan. The sensation coming from her center was all consuming. Tommofey's legs let go of hers and she found herself spreading her legs wider and raising her knees. The prince stopped kissing her and removed his hand, causing Aviva to growl. He climbed in between her legs and kissed her on the stomach, one of his hands massaging her inner thigh.

Tommofey kissed and licked his way down her stomach and over her mound until he reached her clit where his tongue now began to flick up and down, making Aviva groan loudly. She felt his hand slide down her thigh and come to rest at her entrance. Slowly he pushed a finger into her, before drawing it back out and then sliding back in.

Aviva was filled with sensations as the constant pressure from his tongue and the stroking of her insides combined to make her body still and stiffen as if she was hanging on to the edge of a cliff. It was exquisite. And then she was falling, her body shaking with a tremor that spread out from her center.

He removed his hand as the feelings subsided and gently kissed his way back up her torso stopping at each nipple to flick with his tongue before he reached her mouth. "Ready?" he said against her mouth. And it was only then did she realize there was pressure against her entrance.

"Yes." Aviva reached up and fisted his hair, kissing him deeply as he pushed slowly inside her. He pulled out and then pushed in again, moving deeper an inch at a time. The feeling of him inside her was wondrous and she began to raise her hips to meet his every time he entered her.

Tommofey moaned into her mouth, and she smiled knowing that he was enjoying himself as much as she was. Aviva lifted her legs to wrap them around his waist, forcing him deeper inside her. There was a moment of sharp pain and then it was gone. She bit her lip to stop from crying out, but he stilled, knowing somehow what had happened.

"Don't stop," she whispered. Aviva pushed her feet into his gorgeous arse while raising her hips up. Her intention clear.

"You are magnificent." He kissed her forehead, then nose and finally her mouth.

Tommofey started to rock against her and Aviva began to feel the tingling sensation again. The constant rubbing on her clit as he pushed inside her, filling every inch of her was making her pant and arch her back. It was so close. That moment of release was building and it was sublime. How did people get anything else done?

Aviva closed her eyes and pulled hard on Tommofey's hair, making him grunt as she arched her back further and stilled as her orgasm engulfed her. She felt as if she was spiraling, her body clenched around him, and then she felt the prince still on top of her before he too shivered. There was a strange sensation as if he was twitching inside her. As she clenched around him his cock twitched harder and Tommofey swore loudly, before he lay down on top of her breathing heavily.

They lay like that for several moments, enjoying the aftermath of their love making.

"I thought you said you were inexperienced," she accused, breaking the silence.

"That doesn't mean I don't know what I am doing."

"Clearly," she said sarcastically.

Tommofey moved up onto his elbows. "I think the shirt you peeled off me earlier is still on the edge of the bed. Stay still while I get it, okay?"

Aviva was confused, but did what she was told. "Sure."

Slowly Tommofey pulled out of her and she almost cried out when he left her completely and she felt his absence. He lifted himself off her and Aviva missed the weight of him immediately. She did what she was told and didn't move.

"Here," he said as he returned to her side. "Put this between your legs for now. There may be some slight bleeding and no one wants to sleep in the wet spot so hold it there for a few moments. I'll get up and get you a cloth and water in a little while."

Aviva frowned at what he had just said but did what she was told and placed the shirt between her legs. It stung but it was bearable.

Tommofey climbed in beside her again, but this time he moved her, so she was lying on her side, facing away from him. He wrapped his arms around her and pulled her toward him. Surprisingly, to be lying in the prince's arms with him curled around her was the most natural thing in the world.

He lifted her hair and kissed the back of her neck, making her shiver against him. Aviva felt his cock twitch. Could he be ready to do it again so soon? Both Nikkitta and Lyubbov had said their men had fallen asleep almost immediately once they had finished. Aviva was sore, but the thought of him inside her, touching her, kissing her made her push back her hips and grind into him. She could feel his cock grow.

Prince Tommofey continued to kiss the back of her neck as he pushed against her in response. "My Lady, are you sure you are ready for round two?" he asked between kisses.

"Now I know what all the fuss is about, I hope you have plenty of stamina." She giggled and pushed her hips back again.

"Ha, I am eighteen. I have all the stamina you will ever require."

"Promises, promises," Aviva managed to say before he rolled her over and kissed her.

Chapter 17

Aviva

The tent was warm, and Aviva had no intention of ever moving. It was still dark outside, but she could hear the movement of the soldiers as they began to pack up camp. She tried not to dwell on the fact that they now all had to get up a full turning earlier because her illness had kept them from traveling. The heaviness of Tommofey's arm holding her brought Aviva fully awake and she sat up suddenly.

"Hey," the prince grumbled as he rubbed his eyes and looked up at her.

Aviva gathered her blanket up to cover as much of her nakedness as she could.

Tommofey grinned at her and reached out to run his hand down her arm. "Bit late for that, don't you think?"

Slowly, Aviva unclenched her fists and tried to relax. She smiled gingerly at him.

"Sorry, not used to waking up next to a prince," she commented.

He drew her back down to him so she rested on his chest.

"I thought in this little room we were only Aviva and Tommofey?"

She listened to his strong heartbeat and took a few deep breaths. Aviva had no idea why she had woken up and reacted that way; perhaps she had thought he would banish her back to her brother's tent once he had used her. *You're not thinking straight,* she told herself. *If nothing else, he still needs a Servant. The man has no clue how to care for himself.* Aviva sat back up again. *Lying here is not helping, you are going to make yourself upset about nothing,* she warned, having her own private battle in her mind.

"We should get up," she spoke. "I have to pack our things and the men will be waiting to break down the pavilion."

Tommofey made a face at her.

"I don't like it when you make sense."

"Someone has to," Aviva retorted, back on comfortable ground.

"Fine. But today you ride next to me, not back with the Servants and Commoners."

She hid her relief with a mocking incline of her head. "As you wish, My Lord."

Aviva climbed out of bed and poked her head out of the side of her bedchamber curtain, only to giggle as she looked down to find the prince's ankles and feet sticking out under the fabric. He didn't fit in her bed at all, and yet he hadn't tried to make her move to his larger and longer bed in the middle of the pavilion.

"What?" he asked.

"You don't fit."

"I don't fit in most normal spaces. Probably one of the only perks of being born royal is I can afford to have everything adapted to what I need."

Aviva checked again to make sure there were no guards as she stood and quickly moved from her bed chamber to the dressing room next to it, gathering up the clothes they had discarded the night before as she went. Viv quickly dressed and hid her hair under a large kerchief, singing softly to herself as she began to fold and pack away her own clothes before starting on Tommofey's.

He joined her in the dressing room, and she quickly helped him dress before pushing him out the door.

"Excuse me," he huffed as he tried to kiss her, but she turned her head and kept pushing on his chest.

"You kiss me, and we are both going to end up naked. I have caused enough trouble."

"I like being naked with you," he whispered, but allowed her to move him out the way.

It didn't take her long to complete the packing, and by the time she emerged from the dressing room, the main pavilion area had been stripped of his bed, the small crate side table, the stools they had used last night as well as his table that he drew his maps on. The special leather case was nowhere to be seen and the rugs were being rolled up.

Aviva quickly moved to her own bed chamber, leaving the dressing room curtain open so they knew they could start to pack everything into the cart. She folded the blankets and found the soiled shirt he had insisted Aviva use the night before. It was light enough now for her to see the small amount of dried blood on it. Screwing the shirt up and folding it within her blankets, she resolved to wash it while she bathed the next night. She didn't need the gossiping of the Servants who laundered the prince's clothes.

Finally, she was done, and she moved outside the tent completely, so the men could swarm over it and in less than a quarter turning have it packed up. Shai walked up to Aviva who was leading his and her horses. His eyes were bleary and he mumbled a good morning.

"You don't look like your early night did you good," she commented smartly as she took Pepper's reins.

He blinked at her and grunted. "Aren't you chipper this morning?"

The men were forming up to leave and Aviva hesitated a moment. She knew Tommofey had ordered her to ride with him, but she didn't feel comfortable nudging Pepper up next to Toby.

"Good morning, Shai," a voice from behind her spoke. "Did you sleep well?" the prince asked.

This gave Aviva the chance to mount Pepper.

"No," Shai grumbled. "But you look obscenely refreshed." He mounted his own horse, patting its neck to help settle her. "Both of you are too bright and cheery; I am going to sulk elsewhere." And with that he pulled on the reins and guided his horse further back in the line.

Tommofey turned back to smile at her. "Are you ready to ride, Lady Aviva?"

"Yes, Your Highness."

"Good, you may ride beside me today if your brother does not wish your company."

She groaned in protest for the benefit of those around her, but secretly was pleased that he had followed through on his request and had given her a reason for being there. As everyone fell into formation and Aviva took her place next to the prince, there was a muttering from the front of the group. The soldiers moved to either side to allow whoever it was coming through until they reached the prince. It was a small squad of six men with two extra horses being used as pack animals. They wore the same uniform as the men around her. These were the prince's personal soldiers. Why were they here?

The lead man bowed deeply but remained in his saddle. "Your Highness, I have come on the orders of Lady Darria."

Aviva held her breath. What did Tommofey's mother want? No matter how fondly he thought about her, or how good and kind she was in the past, Aviva didn't think highly of the woman.

"Concerning?" Tommofey asked.

"Prince Harlonngraith."

Everyone stilled for a moment. Captain Albertinne nudged his horse forward at the same time that Shai re-joined them.

"Go on," Prince Tommofey ordered.

"Your brother turned up several months ago with a woman, which looked to be of Pomaikkan descent. They tried to keep it secret but there was an issue when they neared the Settlement and the prince revealed himself.

As soon as we got word, this squad was dispatched to investigate. We learned little, but enough to warrant us to leave half of us at the Settlement to keep watch while the rest of us made toward the Arena. I knew in which direction you were headed, so I knew in which way you would be approaching and thought going through the forest would be the quickest route."

"And what did you find out?" Tommofey's tone was light, but Aviva could see the strain around his hazel eyes in the pre-dawn light. His hands clenched the reins of Toby a little tighter than they had mere moments ago.

Her heart went out to him.

"Prince Harlonngraith has found his Champion. She is the Pomaikkan woman."

The prince was lost in his thoughts and Aviva had so many questions. The morning had dawned and the small group of soldiers had joined the rest of the men as they made their way to the Arena. Aviva couldn't hold her tongue any longer and blurted out her questions. "Can the Champion be a woman?"

"Yes. There is no restriction on gender. As you know, a woman can wear the Warrior brand, it is just highly unusual." It was Captain Albertinne who answered.

"Is it odd that she is a Roamer?"

"The correct term is Pomaikkan," muttered the prince.

"Whatever," Aviva snipped back. "Is it odd?"

Again, it was the captain who answered. "It's probably the only way she could be good enough to be Harlonngraith's Champion."

Aviva scowled. This conversation was going nowhere. "What is that supposed to mean? I don't exactly know much about the Pomaikka." She said the word slowly. "We are too remote to get many who visit us."

Her scowl deepened as she watched the prince and his captain exchange a look, but not answer her. She went to open her mouth, but Shai spoke into the silence. "It is well rumored that the Pomaikkan's are gifted fighters in hand-to-hand combat, as well as the staff. King Tommofey sent one of his most promising warriors to learn from them. When he returned, he was the one who taught the king a few new tricks, which is what the king in turn taught me." Shai looked skyward for a moment. "I can't remember the warrior's name, but I do know that King Tommofey admired him and trusted him implicitly."

"His name was Evannderth," Prince Tommofey said quietly.

"Yes." Shai clicked his fingers. "That's the one."

"He married the Pomaikkan Seer, Kahlahnni, and they disappeared a short while later. They haven't been seen since before my birth," the prince explained.

Aviva tried to keep up with all the names and finally it dawned on her. The Seer Tommofey spoke of was the one his mother had imprisoned and the man that had rescued her was the warrior who had been a spy for the Queen.

"Why would Prince Harlonngraith go to the settlement rather than head to the Arena?" she wondered aloud.

"My guess is so his Champion could keep training," Shai said quietly. "It seems that my instinct to train in hand-to-hand combat was warranted."

"You will still have the advantage of being her better with a sword though." Aviva tried to sound encouraging. The idea of him having to hurt someone or be hurt still did not sit well with her. She just wanted the whole thing over so they could settle onto the farm and live out her days caring for horses and not worrying about being someone's property.

"It looks like the Pomaikkans have made their choice in who they want to rule," the prince said to no one in particular. He looked to his side and met Aviva's eyes. "Though to be fair, I think most people want Harlonngraith because he is first born and there is no issue with his parentage."

"But there are people loyal to you," Captain Albertinne interjected pointedly.

Prince Tommofey smiled at his captain. "Yes, because they remember my mother and how kind and brave she was. But be honest, the nobles and rich merchants who have taken my side are all doing so for their own greed."

"Why do it then?" Aviva asked. "Why go through with it?"

Everyone looked at her, though no one seemed too shocked at her outburst.

"To honor my mother and the sacrifices she made."

Aviva held her tongue. The woman was power-hungry and out for revenge and was prepared to sacrifice her son's happiness for it. She bit the inside of her lip to stop from saying anything and insulting the men around her.

"Your face says you don't agree," commented the prince, his hazel eyes wary.

She shrugged. "It is not my place to judge the Lady Darria."

This brought a short laugh from Tommofey. "It may not be your place, but when has that ever stopped you?"

Shai and Captain Albertinne joined in the laughter.

"Fine," she said tartly, "I think it strange that you say she is the one making the sacrifices when I don't see her stepping into the Arena. But I am sure she will be the one standing next to you gloating when Prince Harlon-ngraith's Champion surrenders to my brother."

"There will be no surrender," Tommofey said quietly.

"What? Why?" Aviva had no idea what he meant by that.

"It is a fight to the death."

"Whose death?" she asked, confused.

"Mine and Shai's," Prince Tommofey's voice was sad. "Or my brother's and his Champion."

Aviva halted her horse and looked from the prince to her brother and back again.

"Did you know about this?" she asked Shai.

"Of course."

"Why did you not tell me?"

"I thought you knew."

"You thought I was fine with you fighting to the death?" she screamed at him.

"I'm sorry, Viv, I truly didn't think about it too hard. I figured we were all confident that I would win, so no one brought it up."

"That may be the stupidest thing I have ever heard," she yelled again. "You are putting your life on the line for a god damn farm."

"No," Shai said softly, "I am putting my life on the line so you can be free and happy."

Chapter 18

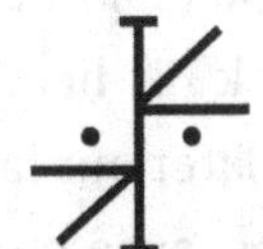

Tommofey

"She won't talk to me." Shai hiccupped as he spoke.

"Me neither," Tommofey said as he looked in his cup, astounded to find it empty. "She disappears each night once I have eaten and I have no idea where she goes. She sneaks back in when she thinks I am asleep, and is dressed and packed before I get up in the morning." He almost said that he missed her but managed to stop himself in time. Tommofey had no idea how Shai would react to that revelation.

"Viv is hiding with the horses," Shai answered.

"The horses," Tom repeated like he was a moron. His brain didn't seem to be working properly. He picked up the small barrel of mead Shai had arrived with and poured them both another drink. Perhaps that would help him see more clearly.

"Yes, she has always done that, ever since our mother died. I think the urge to be around non-people grew more when she was branded a Servant. It was a shock to everyone who knew her, and between you and I, I don't think she ever fully recovered." Shai took a long swig of his mead. "Viv is so smart; she learned to read and write much quicker than I did. She is good with numbers and should have been given the chance to do whatever she wanted, but the Gods had other plans. I will never understand it." He shook his head. "The Gods took our mother and then a year later our father. We were allowed to live in the garrison because our father died in battle, but it was no place for a young girl to grow up. All that bluster and outspokenness hides a terrified little girl who is scared to fall in love in case that person is taken from her too."

Tommofey was silent as he took in all that Shai had revealed about his sister. His heart ached for the young girl she had been and the broken woman she now was.

"Shit, and here I am offering you her chance at happiness while also terrifying her with taking away the only thing she loves." The prince thought about it. "I should be making her life easier, not harder. That's what a real king does." He took a gulp of the mead and pulled a face at the taste. It was no red wine.

"I thought I was doing the right thing," Shai said, draining his glass. He stood and knocked over the stool. Clumsily, Shai picked it up while Tommofey tried to wave him away, someone else could do that. "I am off to bed," his Champion announced.

"A wise decision." Tommofey nodded sagely, almost falling off his own stool. "Thank you for the fine mead and conversation."

Shai bowed and almost toppled over; he stumbled several steps forward before he righted himself. "Yes, definitely time for bed."

Tom watched the man who was willing to fight and die for him just to make his sister happy stagger out of the tent.

"Can someone make certain my Champion makes it safely back to his tent?" he called, frowning as his words slurred.

"Yes, sir," came the quick response.

Prince Tommofey picked up the cup and looked at the mead and decided he could not take another mouthful. Instead, he stood and walked to his bed just a few feet away. He flopped down, not bothering to take his clothes or boots off. The soft light of the two lanterns cast long shadows along the dark blue of his pavilion roof, and his mind wondered what shadows Aviva and he would cast if they were to make love in this light. It felt like a lifetime ago since he had touched her.

The thought of her naked beneath him made his cock harden, but he knew from experience that he had had too much to drink to do anything about it at the moment. The previous night he had lay in bed pretending he was asleep until she had returned safe. Aviva had snuck in and gone straight to her bed chamber, extinguishing the lanterns as she went. Once plunged into darkness, and knowing she was close but untouchable, Tommofey had taken hold of his cock and stroked it, pumping hard and fast as he thought about Aviva under him, panting and begging for him to kiss her. Tonight he would endure his erection without release, just as he deserved.

The idea of losing Shai must be overwhelming, he thought, and a tightness pulled at his chest. He was causing her so much pain. *Maybe I shouldn't go through with it? There is still time to stop it; all I need to do is not turn up. Now where had that thought come from? Mother would be furious, but do I care?*

There were so many thoughts circling in Tommofey's mind that he felt like the room was spinning. Was he really considering not arriving at the most important moment of his life? He was the one who had issued the stupid Challenge. Could he just walk away from it? *You are being ridiculous. Of course, you are going to go. You are just nervous. You were born to be king.* His mind circled back. *What about Aviva? She's a big girl and I care for her, but I am sure once her brother wins and I am crowned king, she will forgive me.*

A tiny voice in the back of his mind whispered just as he closed his heavy eyes. *But what happens if she never forgives you?*

Aviva

The beautiful horse with its braided white mane leaned into the scratches behind her ear.

"You're a good girl," Aviva told her as she bent her head and touched her forehead to Pepper's velvety nose.

It had been two days since Aviva had learned the truth of the Challenge Prince Tommofey had issued to his brother, and she still wavered between feeling blood-boiling angry and sickened with what could go wrong. She had returned to the role of Servant and refused to speak to the prince, other than to ask a direct question about his needs. Shai had tried to engage her in several conversations, but she looked through him and turned away saying she had things to do. She was furious at both of them and wasn't about to let it go.

It didn't matter how she looked at it, the situation was unfair. And Aviva felt guilty. So incredibly guilty. This was all her doing. If she didn't complain so frequently, perhaps her brother would never have felt the pressure to go through with the tournament. It was her dream to own the farm and hide from the world. Now she thought about it, Aviva wasn't even sure her brother wanted it for himself and was only doing it to make her happy. It seemed that he was focused on making her life as comfortable as possible while she had forced him into the whole situation. Maybe it was the Gods punishment for her interfering in their plans. After all, the morning of the tournament he had been safely in jail from fighting with the prince's men the night before. If Aviva had not done what she does best and ignore those around her he would have missed the tournament entirely and he would be safe.

Her thoughts turned away from Shai and refocused on Tommofey. Her feelings for him were even more confusing. She had spent the last two days trying not to run to him and kiss him, begging for him to hold her and touch her. Prince Tommofey was brilliant, quick-witted, gifted, and well-educated, but he was terrible with people. He was rude, arrogant, and thoughtless and never willing to accept his fault in a situation. She was also falling in love with him. But Aviva was struggling with it, as how could she find peace with a man who was willing to allow others to die for his mother's desires?

"What do you think I should do?" she asked Pepper.

The mare nudged her and snuffled at her coat pocket, making Aviva laugh.

"Ha, greedy girl," she teased as she pulled the apple from her pocket. "Is this what you are after?"

Pepper whinnied and bobbed her head.

"Here you go then." Aviva held out the apple on her flattened palm. "I don't know if he'll make a good king," she spoke softly to the horse. "Is that wrong of me?"

Pepper continued to chew, not really interested in Aviva and her problems.

"Is this my fault? I keep thinking if I hadn't forced Shai in the first place we wouldn't be here, but really, Shai is a soldier and he could die in a battle every time he goes back to Pluddgish." She sighed dramatically as Pepper wandered away.

"It seems no one wants to hear me complain." Toby looked up from where he was chewing the grass and walked toward her.

"Hey boy," she said as she reached out to pat him. "Glad someone cares." She gave Pepper's rear end a hard glare.

"You want the truth?" Aviva whispered to Toby. "I'm scared. What if Shai doesn't fight? Pynnan will surely take his place, and will the Gods accept the replacement and allow them into the Arena or will Tommofey be killed for turning up with a false Champion? But what happens if Shai fights and wins and Segarris ends up with a weak king, whose mother is still seeking revenge and does more damage than good to innocent people?" Aviva paused and a single tear slid down her cheek. She rubbed her face on the soft fur of Toby. "Or what happens if Shai loses and I lose the only two people that mean anything to me? I will be forever alone." With her fears finally spoken, Aviva began to sob into the neck of the horse who seemed to understand her need and turned his head toward her, as if giving her a hug with his majestic long neck. This just made Aviva cry harder.

Chapter 19

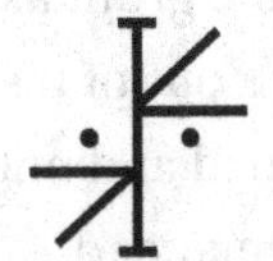

Tommofey

He didn't know what woke him, but Prince Tommofey wished it would go away. He felt awful. He tried to roll over and go back to sleep, but the room was spinning too much, and he felt violently ill. Tom wondered what time it was. How many turnings did he have before he had to get up and ride? The thought made him feel sicker, if that was even possible.

I need water, he thought to himself. He opened his eyes to find someone had extinguished the two lanterns that were typically in the main bed chamber space. Tommofey heard the faintest sound of movement. It must be Aviva. Was she the one who had shut off the lanterns? He went to speak but hesitated—she's not talking to you, remember?

There was another faint rustle of cloth. *What was she doing?* Tom lay there for a few moments longer wrestling with himself. *This is just stupid. She has to talk to me. How long can she hold a grudge?* Tommofey's mind didn't answer...he knew the response to that question. *Forever.*

Deciding to use the excuse that he needed water as to why he got up rather than he wanted to speak to Aviva, Tommofey rolled out of bed. He hit something unexpected and heard a masculine grunt as a person fell over him. This brought the prince out of his haze as he completed the roll out of the low bed and onto the floor.

"Who's there?" he demanded.

The person didn't respond. Instantly the hairs on Tommofey's arms prickled. Something was wrong. Dreadfully wrong.

Think, he told himself. *Cause a distraction, yell for help, and make for the door.* Sounded simple enough, but what could he use for a distraction? Tommofey got up on his knees and grabbed the first thing he thought of—the bedding. They didn't come away easily, so he assumed the intruder was still on the bed where he had fallen. Tom flung the blankets forward in the hope the man would become tangled in them long enough for the prince to run for it.

"Help!" he yelled as he crawled around the bed. He decided not to stand, he was a bigger target standing. "Guard!"

No one came rushing in—this was not a good sign. What was happening?

Abruptly, the night was filled with people yelling and a strange orange glow started to flicker near the doorway. Something was on fire.

Trying to keep his panic under control, Tommofey's thoughts went to Aviva. Where was she? Had she come back? Tom changed direction, and instead of crawling toward the open tent flap he crawled toward her bed chamber. He had to make certain she was safe.

There was a noise coming from his bed area, but he couldn't figure out what it was as the noise coming from outside was too loud. People were yelling and the horses sounded frantic. There was a spark in the darkness that made Tommofey stop for a moment before he started crawling quicker. That had been a flash from a flint being struck. Tom guessed that someone was trying to set a fire in his pavilion. He had to make sure Aviva wasn't in here.

A second spark and the bed caught fire. The sound he couldn't make out before must have been some sort of fluid being poured onto the blankets as they caught fire ferociously. A warm red and orange light filled the room, allowing Tommofey to see a black clad figure with a face wrapping, holding a long, curved sword. *Assassin*, was the first thing that came to his mind.

Being on the ground, on all fours, was most assuredly a disadvantage at this point so Tommofey scrambled to his feet. As he stood, he picked up the small stool. It wasn't a great weapon but it was something to hold.

"Aviva?" he shouted, no longer needing to worry about the intruder finding him. The fire made hiding impossible.

The assassin stalked toward him; his sword held expertly. The scene behind him unfolded as if the Gods had slowed down time. The flames leapt from the bed and into the canvas of the tent, rapidly moving up the wall. Smoke quickly filled the space.

Panic began to fill Tommofey as he thought of several things at once. The fire had now reached the tent entrance, effectively cutting off any means of escape, but also rescue. This was not good. He still didn't know what was happening outside—was the camp under attack? Is that why his guards had not responded? And most importantly, where was Aviva?

He was almost to Aviva's bed chamber curtain when the assassin launched his attack, rushing at Tommofey, his sword held high. *So, this is how I die and my brother gets the throne?* The sword descended and the prince raised the stool, closing his eyes and hoping for the best. The wood shattered and his arms jerked at the downward pressure on the impact.

Tommofey felt a tugging force and opened his eyes to find the sword blade embedded in the seat of the stool. Instead of pulling away he used his superior height and brought what was left of the stool downward, pushing the assassin off balance.

Before Tommofey could congratulate himself for being clever, the assassin dropped to his knees, pulling the prince forward. They both lost their balance and ended up on the floor. All the prince could do was to think to roll away and get to the bed chamber. The smoke was so thick that his eyes were watering, and more than half the pavilion was on fire—and he still didn't know if Aviva was safe.

Coughing and holding the front of his nightshirt to his mouth, Tommofey began to stand when the assassin flipped over and picked up the sword with the stool seat still on its blade and threw it at Tommofey. It hit his thigh and knocked him down again. The assassin was on him, punching him in the face hard. Before he could react to anything other than the pain, the black clad man's hands were around Tom's throat.

The prince bucked and clawed at the hands, but the man's grip was becoming tighter instead of looser. The assassin's eyes were gray like a summer storm with a look of feral determination that Tommofey found oddly fascinating. His thoughts were becoming disjointed, and Tommofey found himself losing consciousness. He fought to keep his eyes open, but his vision was narrowing and his final thoughts were of Aviva and how he would never know if she was safe.

A gush of blood came from the assassin's mouth and covered Tommofey as the man slumped down on top of him.

"My Lord, can you walk?" Albertinne stood over the body of the assassin, a small blood-covered sword in his hand. He bent down and kicked the body off before offering the prince his hand.

It took Tommofey several attempts to speak before any words came out. His voice was hoarse when he finally managed to make a sound. "Can't leave, have to get..." He didn't have the chance to finish. Another figure came into view.

"It's okay, I got it." And there Aviva stood, surrounded by fire and smoke and holding up his leather case.

Chapter 20

Aviva

Aviva sat on the cold ground, her back against the rough bark of the tree. Her nerves were shot, and it was only now that her head had finally stopped pounding from the knock she had received. Last night had been a blur of terror, fire, and blood. It had happened so quickly that she was still processing much of it.

This morning, as the sun had risen to reveal the carnage of the night before, all she could think of was Shai and Tommofey and her secret feelings of guilt for running to check on the prince rather than to see if her brother was safe. Aviva had spent the day justifying her behavior by telling herself that it was logical that the assassins had been after the prince rather than one soldier in his squad. I mean, who really knew which one of these men was Tommofey's selected Champion?

They had buried the five dead, who had fought bravely protecting their prince, and had taken stock of the damage. All but two tents had been destroyed and half of the horses spooked, though most hadn't gone far, and several had wandered back to camp by the morning. After much reporting and discussion, it was decided that there had been three assassins sent. Two created the distraction by releasing the horses and setting the tents on fire after taking out the sentries, while the third had killed the two guards assigned to Tommofey before sneaking in to kill him.

Aviva had been with the horses when it had begun and an assassin had snuck up and hit her on the head, knocking her out. She had come to with Pepper standing over her and flames filling the night sky. Her first thought had been of Tommofey, and Aviva had struggled to her feet and headed in the direction of his tent. She never wanted to experience that wave of despair again when she had seen his tent ablaze and the bodies of his guards sprawled across the entrance. It was at that moment that she had spotted someone cutting a hole in the pavilion fabric, and through the haze of smoke, Aviva couldn't make out who it was. Putting all caution aside, she had run for the man only to find it was Albertinne stepping into the dressing room. She didn't hesitate to follow.

Aviva felt the gentle nudge of Pepper trying to get her attention, which brought her out of her memories. Grateful for the distraction, Aviva stood and brushed off the dirt of the ground.

"How are you doing, girl?" she asked the beautiful beast.

It had become almost a ritual for Aviva to find solace amongst the horses at the moment. They didn't demand anything but pats and the occasional snack from her, unlike their human riders. Toby huddled against the other side of Aviva, and she reached out to caress him with her other hand. "It was a bit scary last night, wasn't it?" she said.

"It really was," a voice answered. It was Tommofey.

Aviva ignored him. She was still angry at him for keeping the details of the Right to Rule battle to himself. He had still not apologized, and now she was unreasonably angry with him for scaring her so much the night before and that she had run to him instead of Shai. Aviva had no desire to examine those feelings and thoughts too deeply, not liking what it meant, so she had simply decided to take it out on him by continuing to ignore him.

"The stew was a little burnt tonight, wasn't it?" he spoke to Toby in a conversational tone.

Aviva bit her tongue to stop herself from replying to him directly. She stood mutely in between Pepper and Toby.

The prince continued with his one-way conversation. "I am not looking forward to sleeping on the hard ground tonight and I probably won't fit in the tiny tent."

"Can you shut up," she exploded at him, startling the horses surrounding them and herself.

Tommofey blinked at her and closed his mouth.

"No one cares, you ungrateful sod," Aviva snarled, all her pent-up fear and rage directed at Tommofey. "People died to protect you last night, my brother is willing to enter an arena and fight to the death for you, and all you can do is complain that your food was slightly burnt and that you have to sleep on the ground in a small tent." She took in a huge breath in the hope it would calm her. It didn't.

"In my opinion, you are too selfish to be a good king. You don't deserve it." Aviva spun around and stomped away. She couldn't bear to be near him and his appalling attitude. So many men buried in the forest, never to return to their loved ones because his mother wanted him to be king. It was revolting. All this waste when they could have a happy life traveling around and mapping out Segarris. The thought stopped her mid-stride—now where had that come from? Aviva shook her head and kept walking. It doesn't matter where the thought came from, it didn't matter if she loved him, he was infuriating and selfish.

"Who's there?" a voice called, which stopped her with a jolt of fright. She had reached the edge of the camp without realizing it.

"Sorry, it's just Aviva." She peered into the darkness, a shape moved away from the tree.

"Lady Aviva, you need to return to the firelight, it may not be safe out here."

"It's fine, I will take her back." Prince Tommofey came to stand beside her.

The dark figure bowed. "I did not realize you were with her, My Lord."

"I don't see how you couldn't with all the shouting at me she has been doing."

"I was attempting to be polite," the soldier answered.

"I appreciate it," the prince joked, and Aviva scowled at him, only then realizing he couldn't see her.

"I'll keep the shouting down," she told the guard on sentry duty and turned to walk back to the camp.

Prince Tommofey followed.

"What are you doing? Go away." Aviva was still irritated and didn't need him following her.

"No. You heard him; it isn't safe out here by yourself."

She huffed at him and walked a few more steps before stopping. They now stood amongst the trees, out of sight of everyone—the horses between them and the camp-fires and curious eyes. Aviva's temper was beginning to cool, and she was now regretting her hastily shouted words. They had been harsh for no other reason than to hurt him, but there was no way she was going to let him know that. She felt guilty and sad.

Tommofey

"I was terrified last night." He spoke quietly. "I couldn't find you. There was smoke and fire and people shouting, and a man trying to kill me, and all I could do was think about you and if you were safe."

"When I saw our tent on fire, I was so scared," she whispered, her eyes filling with tears. "People were running everywhere, and then I saw Albertinne cut the wall to get to you and I followed. I had to know if you were alive."

"Thank you for saving my cartography case."

"I know how important it is to you."

"Never as important as you are."

Tommofey reached out and hesitantly took her hands. He wasn't sure of how she would react. She didn't pull away. He brought her hands up to his face and deliberately turned her hands over, exposing the Servant brand on her left wrist. "I will forever be your servant. Whatever you wish that is in my power to grant, I will."

He brought his lips down to her wrist and kissed the brand.

"I will never understand how the Gods did this to you. You are so clever and capable. How many other Servants are out there who should never have had this brand? As king, I could maybe find out how the branding works and hopefully do something about it."

"You would do that?" she asked.

"Yes. The Servant brand, as far as I understood, was only ever supposed to be for those who weren't capable of protecting themselves. It was a way for the nobles and more wealthy people to provide for those less able to."

She looked up at him through her dark lashes and his heart raced. Her brown eyes clear in their want.

"I am sorry I called you selfish and said you wouldn't make a good king."

"You weren't wrong. I do put my wants over others' needs and it is something I have to work on. I need you with me to point it out." Tommofey let go of her hands and lifted his hand to gently pull the kerchief from her head, watching her gorgeous brown curls tumble around her face. "I just hope you can point it out a tad quieter in the future."

She gave him an earnest look. "That does not seem to be an unreasonable request." Aviva reached out and drew her finger along his jawline. "Though, you and I both know it might take me some practice in remembering it."

This made him chuckle softly.

"We could both use some practice of being aware of how our words affect others it seems."

"Do you really expect me to respond to that?" Aviva smirked up at him and Tommofey's heart lifted. Maybe there was a chance for them, but what did that really mean? "What are we doing?" she asked, echoing his thoughts.

"Have you turned into a mind reader?" he asked.

"Why?"

"I was just thinking the same thing."

"Oh, and do you have an answer?"

"I don't know."

"Well, that is exceedingly helpful." Her words rang with sarcasm.

Tommofey placed his fingertip on her lips. "Shhh."

"Make me," Aviva challenged.

"Impossible woman." He smiled and whispered as he bent to kiss her.

Their lips met and Tommofey felt at home. As long as he was with Aviva, he would be a good king. She made everything make sense. Without her he couldn't imagine the cold and lonely life that he would have to endure. The throne had never looked less appealing. He broke off the kiss and held her tightly; he loved the way she tucked in under his chin.

"I was so scared last night," she whispered. "When I saw your tent on fire..." Her voice trailed off. "God, I was so angry at you, and then when I thought you were dead—" She faltered and began to cry softly.

Tommofey held her tightly against his chest, stroking her wonderful curls and making hushing sounds in between kissing the top of her head. "You had every right to be angry," he told her as he listened to her tears subside. "Shai and I were thoughtless and cavalier with your feelings. I know that's how men typically handle things, but we should have considered what it would do to you. The thought of losing Shai, the only constant and reliable person in your life, was something we weren't willing to see."

The prince let Aviva go and took her face into his hands, cupping her jaw. He made her look up at him.

"I can't promise you a happily ever after, but I can promise that I will love you until my last breath."

The words hung between them. He had not planned on telling her how he felt, but now it seemed so important that she know. He wanted her to know she was important to more than just Shai.

"You love me?" He watched her try to understand what he was saying. "Me?"

"Yes, you. My darling, Aviva, you are lovable in so many ways. I couldn't imagine my life without you in it."

"But I am a Servant."

"I don't see how that is relevant to how I feel and what I see when I look at you."

"Loving me is not a wise choice," she pointed out.

"Are you trying to talk me out of my own feelings?"

"No, I just think you should take a moment and think about it. Your father made one hell of a mess, aren't you required to be with someone to mend all the fences?"

"Aviva, can we just not have this week?" Tommofey pleaded. He didn't want to think about anything other than the love he felt at this moment and how she made him want to be better.

"Yes, we can be Tommofey and Aviva for this week." Her voice was sad.

He bent and kissed her softly.

"I will be the court's newly appointed cartographer and you will be my sexy assistant. We have been employed to map the area. All the people we travel with are here to protect us from the wilderness." He created the scenario, secretly wishing it were real.

Aviva reached up and took hold of the front of his shirt. "And I have had to bring my annoying brother along because he always gets in trouble when I am not around." She pulled Tommofey down to her and kissed him deeply, her tongue pushing into his mouth to join with his.

They were both breathing heavily as they broke apart.

"Tommofey..." Aviva sighed, her voice catching at the end. "Don't you dare die. I don't think I could live without you."

He kissed the tip of her nose. "Lady Aviva, I have no intention of dying, but it's good to know you care for me."

"Prince Tommofey, I love you. Even though I want to strangle you more than half the time, I do love you."

"What a charming thing to say," he said sardonically. "You do have a way with words."

"Is there any chance you can stop talking now?" she asked.

He laughed. Loudly. She always said the unexpected. "You," he started to speak but was stopped with her hand being put over his mouth.

"We have one week to be Viv and Tom, and they are far more adventurous than Prince Tommofey and Lady Aviva."

He raised his eyebrows, but she didn't remove her hand to allow him to speak.

"Tom, I want you to push me up against that tree over there and do whatever you want. Do you understand me?" Aviva asked.

He nodded. His cock was already hard with the anticipation of what she had implied.

Chapter 21

Aviva

The Challenger's Arena was massive. A huge, round stone building with many steps leading up to the entrances, hidden away in the thick, lush forest of Saffed. Somehow, against all odds, they had managed to arrive in Central Seggar mere hours after Harlonngraith.

Aviva sat nervously on the end of the prince's bed as she waited for him to finish reporting to his mother and for someone to come and collect her. It turned out that Lady Darria had been the first to arrive two days prior, worried that for some reason she would be blocked from entering the area. *More like paranoid*, Aviva thought. She still hadn't met the woman, and honestly, she wasn't looking forward to it.

Shai sat quietly at the small desk that had replaced Tom's old one, methodically sharpening his sword. The noise of the wet stone sliding over the steel of the blade was somehow soothing to Viv. It reminded her of their father.

"How are you feeling?" she asked her brother, wanting to fill the silence in the room.

"Determined. Responsible." He stopped what he was doing and looked over at her. "How are you feeling?"

"Honestly, I feel sick. There are so many things I can't control at this moment. This waiting is killing me."

"It will all be over tomorrow. No more waiting," he said, ever the pragmatist.

"That was incredibly helpful." Her voice dripped with sarcasm.

"Glad you thought so." He grinned at her before his face became serious. "I am going to ask you this once, and whatever you decide I will do."

Aviva nodded for him to continue.

"If you don't want me to go through with this, now is the time to speak up. Pynnan can step in and take the role of Champion and we can walk away. I did this to make you happy and to give you the freedom the Gods should have. I can't erase your brand, but I can earn us enough money and prestige that you can belong to me in essence and be free to choose your life."

She had known at some point Shai would do this, and Aviva had thought she would be able to answer it without hesitation. She loved Tommofey and Shai was his best chance at surviving whatever tomorrow brought, but now that it was all here, she was unsure. Viv was scared and torn between losing both of them if Shai fought and lost, but losing just Tom if she told Shai not to fight. Something deep inside her knew that regardless of what happened she would lose the prince as they could never marry because of her brand. It was impossible.

"I have been thinking about that since the night of the attack when it all somehow became more real, and in the end, I have decided that this is completely up to you," she answered. "Shai, I love you and am the luckiest girl in the world to have you as my brother, but this is your life and your decision. Whatever you decide I will support."

"Even if I walk away and Tommofey dies because Pynnan is not good enough?" Shai's gaze was direct.

Aviva met his eyes and held them. "Yes. I won't deny that I love the prince, with all his faults, and let's face it, he has many. He is a good man with a bad upbringing. But this is your life. I have no right to tell you what to do."

There was a cough as the guard that stood outside the tent entered.

"You are requested to join Prince Tommofey and Lady Darria in the dining tent. Would you both please follow me?"

"Lead the way," Shai said as he stood and held out his arm to Aviva. She took it and gripped his forearm. "You ready for this?" he asked quietly as they walked out into the dappled sunlight of the forest.

"Are you?" she asked.

"I'm not the one sleeping with her son," he whispered saucily.

"Thanks." Aviva grimaced up at him.

"Don't worry about it. I got you."

Her grimace changed to a soft, genuine smile and her heart hurt a little as she wondered how she ever got so lucky to have a brother who loved her so much. "And I got you."

They were stopped from any further discussion as they were brought to the small navy tent that was being used as the dining tent for the prince and his mother. Tommofey stood before the doorway, being too tall to stand in it. Aviva's heart fluttered at the sight of him. As she and Shai reached his side, he turned and ducked to walk into the tent. They followed.

A tall woman standing about six feet, with long light brown hair, the same color as her son's, stood in the center of the single room. Aviva curtsied and Shai bowed.

"Mother, I would like to introduce you to Shai, the man who will stand as my Champion tomorrow. One of his instructors over the years was my father, which I see as a good omen. This is his sister, Aviva."

"Ah, the Servant you have been sharing your bed with."

Aviva had already surmised that someone would tell the discarded queen what her son had been up to, so did not act surprised. Neither did Tommofey as he spoke clearly. "I also share my heart with her."

This brought a short, derisive laugh from Lady Darria. "This fling ends now."

"You want me to enter that Arena tomorrow and issue my Right to Rule, it will be on my terms, and my term is that Aviva will remain by my side." He reached out and took Viv's hand. "Always. Servant or not, Lady Aviva will be my wife."

Her eyes narrowed at the both of them, and Aviva had to stop herself from shrinking under the piercing stare. She had never felt so intimidated in her life. The words he had spoken barely penetrated. Shai moved to stand in front of Aviva, inserting himself in the conversation.

"You speak to my sister in anything other than a respectful manner and I don't fight for your son. Are we clear?"

Darria looked astounded. Aviva guessed she was not used to anyone, especially her son and a common warrior, speaking to her in such a tone. "Well, it seems your father's stupidity when it comes to women has bred true in you and your brother."

"What's that supposed to mean?" Tommofey asked.

"Rumor is circulating through the camps that Harlonngraith has turned up Bonded to the Roamer who is his supposed choice of Champion."

"**W**hat does Bonded mean?" Aviva asked as they entered Tommofey's new tent.

"It's a Pomaikkan term for married."

"Do you think his mother is as pissed about his choice of partner as your mother is?"

This made Tommofey laugh, dispelling some of the tension. "Yes, possibly more."

"Did you mean it?" she asked. "That you wanted to...you know."

He took her hand and she allowed herself to be drawn into his arms. "Yes, I meant it."

"I think you missed something in the whole process."

He let her go and took a step back. "I did?"

"Tom, you can be so obnoxious sometimes," she ground out the words. "You know you did."

"I wanted to do it right."

"We don't have time for right. There is only right now." She pointed out softly.

He reached out and tucked one of her curls behind her ear; it was one of many habits they had quickly formed.

"Lady Aviva, would you do me the honor of consenting to marrying me?"

"I'll think about it," she joked.

"You'll think about it?" Tommofey raised his eyebrows before he realized she was making fun. "Perhaps I can convince you of my worthiness?"

"How do you plan to do that?" It was Aviva's turn to raise her eyebrows in mock surprise.

He pulled her towards him and kissed her. His soft lips on hers quickly becoming demanding. The fire in the pit of her stomach ignited and she deepened the kiss. The need for him to be inside her, touching her, kissing her, was a constant at the moment. Since the assassin attack they had spent their nights making love and their days in the saddle. It had been exhausting, but beautiful as they came to understand each other on a deeper level.

Aviva didn't bother to take off her layers of skirts, just her breeches and shoes. She needed him now. Taking control of the moment, she pushed Tommofey to the floor. He sat with his legs out in front of him and his back resting against his bed. The look he gave her was one of hunger as he quickly unlaced the front of his pants.

Aviva watched with lust as he took out his cock and firmly stroked it while she stood over him. Her lower stomach tightened in the familiar need she had grown to love, and she gathered her skirts and knelt over her prince, a leg on either side as she lowered herself down and onto his waiting cock.

She let out a gasp of delight and arched her back as he pushed inside her. Aviva ground her hips in the way she had discovered made her clit rub against him. She moved back and forth, keeping the pressure steady and strong as the sensation of him inside her joined with the building orgasm.

Tommofey kissed her neck, running his tongue up to her ear lobe where he gently bit it before he wound his hand in her hair and pulled her head back so he could watch her. "Say yes," he whispered. "Marry me? Please?"

She looked at him, her body tingling and her breath ragged as she teetered on the edge. He grunted as she swirled her hips and tensed her internal muscles. He was at her mercy, and she loved it. She moved quicker, grinding against him harder and faster, her excitement overflowing until it reached its peak. Aviva stilled on top of him for several moments, her body poised in exquisite limbo before she fell. She kissed him hard as she shivered in delight as her orgasm took over all sensible thought. She broke the kiss and locked eyes with him. "Cartographer or king, I will marry you for you." And with those words she moved her hips and clenched her muscles, sending him into his own heady moment.

The beautiful moment passed and Aviva settled against Tommofey's chest, not quite ready to move off him. She tried to savor the feelings, not ready to face the reality of what tomorrow could bring. "Please don't die tomorrow," she whispered, her voice catching at the end as the tears she had been holding back all week finally began to fall.

"Shhh..." He gently stroked her hair. "Let us think about tomorrow when it comes. For the moment, let us be Viv and Tom, and plan our simple wedding."

Aviva knew it was wrong to ignore what tomorrow would bring, but she couldn't help but love him more when he asked. "So, what flowers do you think you would like in your bouquet?"

This story continues in

Betrayal
Right to Rule
Book 4

It's time to decide who has the Right to Rule.

Prince Harlonngraith, and his estranged half brother Prince Tommofey, followed the advice of the Seer and found their Champions. They stand ready to enter the Arena and begin a battle to the death for the Right to Rule the nation of Segarris. The stakes are deadly: the Prince of the vanquished Champion earns immediate death at the hand of his brother.

Betrayals are exposed and alliances will shift as conniving queens and their chosen offspring face the Seer, Kahlahnni, returned, her full powers restored. Lahnni will do what is right for her nation, even if it means sacrificing her child. Can the queens say the same, or is their need for revenge all consuming?

Which prince will get his happily ever after, and who will die?

Excerpt from Betrayal

As blood streamed from his nose, he smiled at her in an oddly charming way. "You are spectacular. Who trained you?"

"I am the daughter of Evannderth," she found herself replying.

"If I had known that I may not have agreed to this."

There was no answer to that.

They circled each other, blades joining in a clatter as they showed again and again how evenly matched they were with this weapon. The crowd had grown quiet, and the tension grew. Everyone waited for a mistake to be made.

The Champions continually changed hands, each showing their prowess, every sword stroke countered until he launched a flurry of rapid overhead swings that forced Marra to raise both her hands to hold the handle of her sword to stop the downward force of his blade, and as they connected with a clash of steel, Marra felt her rib twinge. She tried to keep the grimace from her face, but by the look of triumph in her opponent's eyes, she had not succeeded. He now knew her weak spot.

Warrior Brand

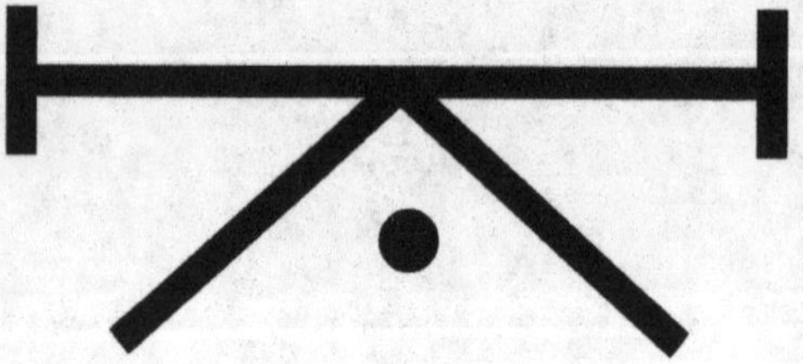

Religious Brand

Servant Brand

Commoner Brand

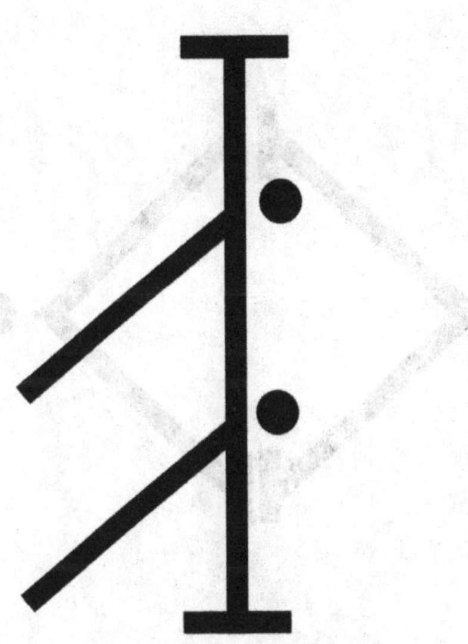

Roamer Brand

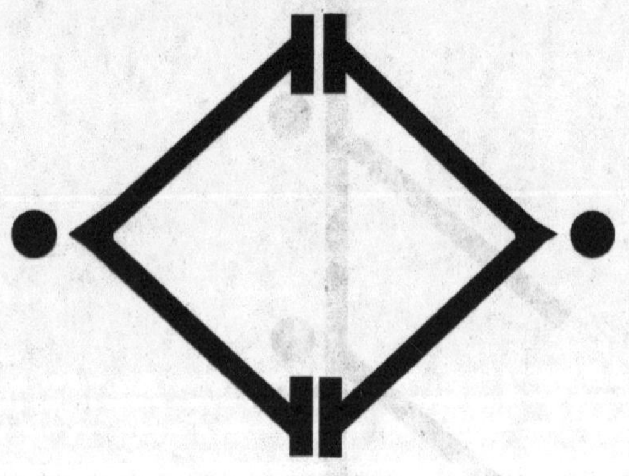

Gifted Brand

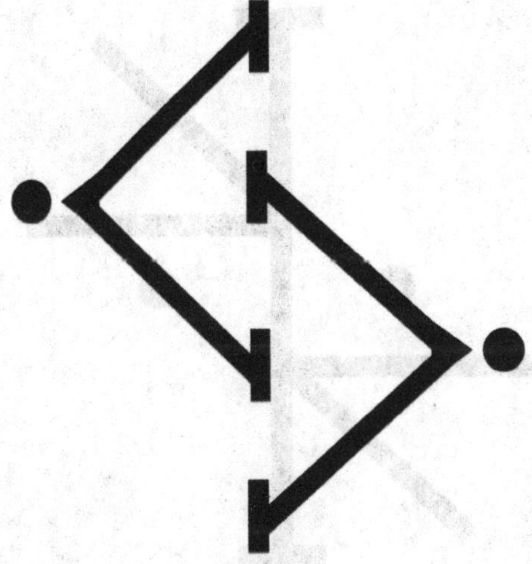

Noble Brand

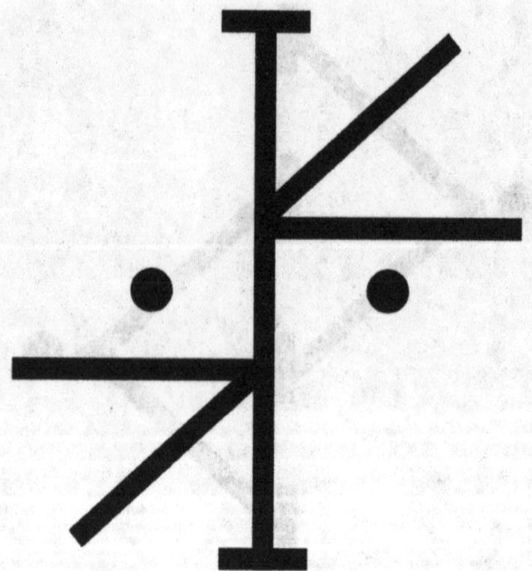

Monarch Brand

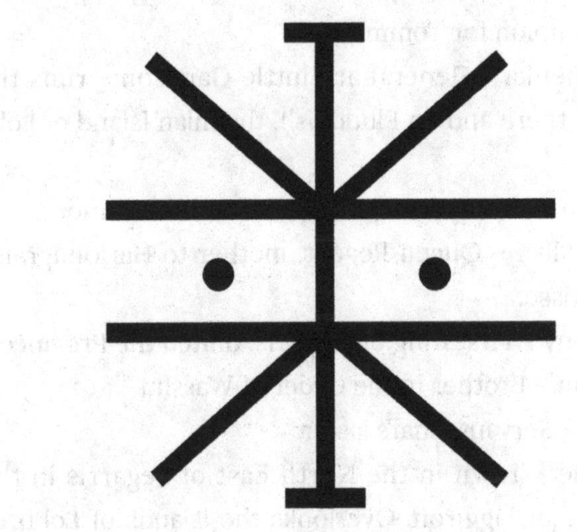

Glossary

Aislynn – Lady of Burrop.

Albertinne (Captain) - Leading the group finding the Champion for Tommofey.

Alloshenka - General at Binttle Garrison - runs the outpost there and on Pluddgish, the mian Island of Lobbregath.

Ambrosse – Boy in orphanage in Gennestenmont.

Anzhellika – Queen Regent, mother to Harlonngraith and Platisse.

Arsenny – First King of Segarris, united the Provinces.

Arttem – Brother in the Order of Wasshu.

Aviva - Servant, Shai's sister.

Binttle - Town in the North East of Segarris in the Province of Jaggiron. Overlooks the Islands of Lobbregath.

Cellecia – Guardian of Kahlahnni. Wife of Emmettin. Mother of Margueritte, Mechelle, and Mattilde.

Channing – Lord of Burrop.

Correntin – Sergeant in Segarrin army.

Csennia – Twin city to Arsenny. Name for the first queen of Segarris.

Daiisi - General Alloshenka's horse.

Dancing Boar - name of an Inn.

Darria – Once Queen, now Lady. Mother to Tommofey.

Darvell - Stablemaster in the garrison of Binttle.

Eltta – Pomaikkan instructor.

Emmettin Finnley – Former Captain in Segarrin navy. Husband to Cellecia, father of Margueritte, Mechelle, and Mattilde. Guardian of Kahlahnni.

Evannderth Durrand – Sergeant, then Captain in the army of Segarris. Bonded to Kahlahnni, father of Samarra.

Fabbron - Drill Sergeant in Brinttle.

Fennkston - Mayor of Binttle.

Griggory - Tommofey's Page.

Harlonngraith – First born son to King Tommofey and Queen Anzhellika.

Heiranni – Pomaikkan instructor for the Gifted. Father to Lopakka.

Innessa – Sister of the Order of Seggar.

Ittaie – General in Segarris army.

Jossiner – Laundry owner in Gennestenmont.

Kahlahnni – Seer of Segarris.

Laurynnse - Groomsman for Prince Tommofey.

Lavee – Brother in the Order of Seggar.

Lopakka – Pomaikkan instructor for the Gifted. Son of Heiranni.

Lyubbov - one of the Servants at Binttle. Roommate of Aviva.

Marggot – Worked in laundry in Gennestenmont.

Margueritte – Eldest child of Cellecia and Emmettin. Sister of Mechelle and Mattilde.

Mattilde – Third born child of Cellecia and Emmettin. Sister of Margueritte and Mechelle.

Mechelle – Second child of Cellecia and Emmettin. Sister of Margueritte and Mattilde.

Nikkitta - one of the Servants at Binttle. Roommate of Aviva.

Ottilie - Housekeeper in charge of Binttle garrison.

Peggy – Evannderth's maid in the palace.

Pepper - Aviva's horse.

Platisse – Second born son to King Tommofey and Queen Anzhellika. Brother of Harlonngraith and Tommofey.

Pynnan - Warrior escorting Prince Tommofey.

Ripperedst - Village in Wasshun Province.

Ruby – Kahlahnni's Horse.

Samarra – Daughter of Kahlahnni and Evannderth. Soul Sleeper of Segarris. Champion to Prince Harlongraith.

Shacram - Disc like weapon attached to a chain. Common to the Islands of Lobbregath.

Shai - Tommofey's Champion. Aviva's brother.

Sittiq – Brother in the Order of Seggar.

Toby - Tommofey's horse.

Tommofey – Former King of Segarris.

Tommofey - Prince of Segarris. Mother - Lady Darris, father - King Tommofey, half brother to Harlonngraith and Platisse.

Tommofey – Third born son to King Tommofey, first born to Lady Darria. Half-brother to Harlonngraith and Platisse.

Traiss – Inn Keeper's daughter in Gennestenmont.

Zussya – Arch Deacon of the Order of Seggar.

About Taya Rune

Taya Rune is a writer of romance, a sucker for happy endings, and has a knack for asking people uncomfortable questions.

She is a USA Today Bestselling Author and a finalist for the 2022 Romantic Book of the Year, for the Romance Writer's of Australia RuBY awards. She has had her work published in many different anthologies and publications.

Romantic Women's Fiction

Reflections of Love Collection

Also releasing on Radish and available in Audio format

Hannah

Samantha

Olivia

Chloe

Lacy

Grace

Reflections of Love Novella Collection Volume 1

(Contains books 1 – 4)

For more information on all titles head to tayarune.com

Acknowledgments

I would like to take a few moments
to say thank you.

To my children, thank you for
teaching me to let go of the small stuff. I am proud of you.

To my family, thank you for the
love and support you have shown me throughout the
years.

To my friends, the ones that have
my back and are forever in my corner – I cherish you.

To my editor, Rochelle J. Simas – IDK art.
Thank you for the kind words that
always accompany the return of my fabulously edited
manuscripts.

To my ARC, Street, Beta, and Proofreader Teams.
You are appreciated.

Follow her on your favorite
platform:

Website:
https://www.tayarune.com

Facebook:
https://www.facebook.com/taya.rune.75

Facebook Group:
https://www.facebook.com/groups/tayasromanticrcal
m

Instagram:
https://www.instagram.com/tayarune/

Bookbub:
https://www.bookbub.com/authors/taya-rune

Goodreads:
https://www.goodreads.com/author/show/21156065.T
aya_Rune

Pinterest:
https://www.pinterest.com.au/TayaRune

Taya Rune